Duffy's Rocks

A John D. S. and Aida C. Truxall Book

Duffy's Rocks

Edward Fenton

Foreword and Afterword by
Margaret Mary Kimmel

GOLDEN TRIANGLE BOOKS

UNIVERSITY OF PITTSBURGH PRESS

Published by the University of Pittsburgh Press, Pittsburgh, Pa. 15261
Copyright © 1999, University of Pittsburgh Press
All rights reserved
Manufactured in the United States of America
Printed on acid-free paper
10 9 8 7 6 5 4 3 2 1

Library of Congress Cataloging-in-Publication data
Fenton, Edward, 1917-
    Duffy's Rocks / Edward Fenton : foreword and afterword by Margaret
Mary Kimmel
    p.   cm.
"Golden triangle books."
    SUMMARY: Feeling imprisoned by life in a grimy town of poor immigrant families
near Pittsburgh during the 1930s, young Timothy Brennan sets out to find his father
who abandoned him many years earlier.
    ISBN 0-8229-5706-X (pbk.)
    [1. Fathers and sons Fiction.   2. Irish Americans Fiction.   3. Pittsburgh (Pa.) Fiction.]
    I. Kimmel, Margaret Mary.   II. Title.
    PZ7.F35 Du 1999
    [Fic]–dc21   99-6464
                                                 CIP

A CIP catalog record for this book is available from the British Library.

The three powers of the soul:
memory,
understanding,
will.

CONTENTS

Foreword

Like those in other parts of the country, Pittsburgh citizens are worried by the Depression, a time when jobs are few and money hard to come by. Timothy Brennan is worried, too. He is afraid he'll never find his father again; Timothy needs to know why his father had left him seven years before, walking out before a promised trip to the circus.

Duffy's Rocks takes place in the 1930s in McKees Rocks. Then, like now, "the Rocks" is a place where hard working families live, seeking a better life for themselves and their children. Timothy lives with his Grandmother, his aunt, and her daughter, his cousin Mary Agnes. His search for his father dominates his life as he and Mary Agnes explore the Pittsburgh of the 1930s from Oakland to the William Penn Hotel. Mary Agnes is shocked and then intrigued by Timothy's ability to find his way about the city, to find a lunch for little more than pennies or a ticket to the Syria Mosque to hear the Pittsburgh Symphony. But on these rambles, Timothy is always watching for his father. On one memorable trip to Pittsburgh, Timothy is sure that he recognizes his father, the debonair Bart Brennan. The man is kind, but assures Timothy that they are not related. The family is cold and unresponsive to Timothy's attempts to find his father. Even Mary Agnes finds Timothy's search useless.

The Brennan family is suspicious of anyone who isn't Irish,

yet they live and work in the diversified community of "the Rocks." Timothy watches churches flash past as he and Mary Agnes ride the streetcar to Pittsburgh, each like part of "a rosary strung across the town with each bead in a different language. There was the German church... then St. Margaret of Hungary; St. Ladislaus, which was Slovak; St. Jan Nepomuk's (Czech; Mrs. Sevchick from next door went there.) After that came ... the Lithuanian church with a saint's name that he couldn't pronounce; St. Josaphat's Ukrainian Catholic Church; Our Lady of Czestochowa, which was Polish; and St. Catherine of Genoa, faced all over with gaudy Italian stonework." The Brennans question the values of other ethnic groups yet share the same worries and work with them. "Imagine eating spaghetti every day," says Aunt Loretta of an Italian friend. Yet when Timothy points out that the Irish eat potatoes everyday, the family sees no similarity at all and are shocked that Timothy would make such a comparison.

This is a story rich in the life of the place and times, yet aching in Timothy's search for who he is. His lonely, scary journey to New York City finalizes the search for the man Timothy longs to know yet never finds. *Duffy's Rocks* is the story of a young boy's coming of age, a character and family one will not easily forget.

Margaret Mary Kimmel

Duffy's Rocks

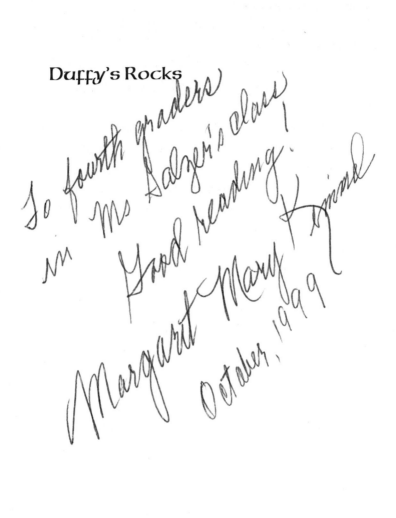

To fourth graders
in Ms Salgen's class)
Good reading!

Margarit Mary Kimmel

October, 1999

ONE

Downtown

The first time Timothy went downtown to Pittsburgh by himself was when Sister Scholastica had arranged for the whole class at St. Bridget's to attend a special program. He couldn't remember afterwards what it had been, exactly: some real live writer from Ireland was giving a talk, something like that. It was going to take place in the Carnegie Library.

He had overslept that day and missed the group. It was Saturday, so he could just as well have stayed home, but he decided to go on his own, anyway. When he got there, he couldn't find his class or the room where the author was supposed to give his talk. He wandered all over the building, looking at the exhibits. Then he went down to the reading room, where he got some books which looked interesting and sat down leafing through them.

After a while he became aware of the man who sat across the table from him, behind a pile of heavy volumes.

His breath caught in his throat. He was positive that it was his father. He kept staring until finally the man became uneasy.

The man set aside his book and smiled self-consciously.

"Is anything the matter, son?" He said it in a kindly voice.

Timothy could feel the blood rushing to his cheeks.

He stammered, "Your—your name's Bart Brennan, isn't it?"

The man, still smiling, shook his head.

Timothy remained unconvinced. He was sure that he had found his father. He kept on steadily regarding him.

The man looked perplexed. Then, reaching into his coat pocket, he said, "Would you like to see my driver's license, so you can be sure?"

Timothy shook his head. Then he got up quickly and walked out of the building, his face blazing with disappointment and shame.

After that he roamed aimlessly. He had a crazy idea that his father was there, somewhere in Pittsburgh. He peered at the faces of all the men he passed to see if any of them might be his father's.

But none of them was.

After a time he began to feel hungry. He was thinking about maybe buying a candy bar, when he found himself approaching a mammoth building with a sign on the front of it which said SYRIA MOSQUE. It had a marquee, which meant that it must be some kind of theatre. There was a crowd outside. Big cars, some of them limousines, were pulling up in front of it.

Timothy crossed the street and stood under the marquee to watch the people going in. Just as he was inching his way toward the posters to read what was going on inside, a woman in a fur coat and a blue velvet hat came up to him.

"Would you like a ticket for the matinee?" she asked him. "I happen to have an extra one." And before he could answer, or say "Thank you," or anything, she had handed it to him and disappeared in the crowd.

He stood there for a couple of minutes, the ticket in his

hand, not sure what to do. Then he got in the line at the door, handed in the ticket, and went inside.

It was warm in the auditorium and the lights were bright. An usher led him to a seat down in the center of the orchestra and gave him a program.

All the people around him were well-dressed, and a lot of them seemed to know each other. The stage was bare. Musicians were walking onto it and settling themselves into their chairs. There was the sound of instruments being tuned, a formless tootling and scraping.

When Timothy finally opened his program he discovered that he was attending a symphony concert. The program notes were rather confusing, with a great many foreign words which he didn't understand, so he set it aside and just waited quietly for whatever was going to happen, and watched the musicians, until the lady in the fur coat came and sat in the seat next to his.

Timothy nodded shyly.

She slipped out of her coat and let it fall over the back of her seat. Timothy thought of reaching out to help her with the sleeves, the way gentlemen did in the movies, but he didn't dare.

"I think," she remarked, as she settled back against her coat and opened her program, "the Maestro has done such wonders with our orchestra, don't you?"

Timothy realized that she didn't really expect an answer. She was reading the program and skimming over all those foreign words. He was sure she understood all of them. He glanced at her out of the corner of his eye. She had on a blue dress and pearls. Her hair was soft gray and her eyes were blue. She smelled nice.

There was a burst of applause as the conductor strode out onto the stage. He had a long Italian name. That didn't surprise Timothy. All classical musicians, he knew, were foreigners.

The hall was filled with a last-minute rustle of programs and whispers. The lights were adjusted. The conductor rapped his stick and raised his arms. The music began.

Timothy didn't know the piece they played. It was something he had never heard before. At first he watched the conductor and the musicians. It was interesting to see what they did, and to hear what kind of sounds came out when they did it. Then his attention began to wander. It was all a jumble of notes to him, but he sat very stiffly, not wanting the lady to think he wasn't appreciating it properly. It went on for a long time.

And then, just as he was beginning to enjoy it, the music ended.

The lights went up. There was to be an intermission, it seemed. The lady smiled at him, got up, and went off to talk to some friends. Timothy stayed in his seat, too nervous to leave it.

The lady didn't come back until the Maestro had already appeared again.

This time Timothy didn't try to follow the music. He just let it flow around him. After a while separate tunes began to emerge from the chaos of sound. The music took on a shape. He didn't have to pretend to appreciate it. He could follow what the different instruments were doing.

When the symphony was over, and the right time came to applaud, and the lights went up, the lady turned to him and said, "Oh, there's just no one like Beethoven, is there? Whenever anyone asks me which of his symphonies is my favorite, I always answer, 'The one I heard last!'" Timothy noticed how the skin around her eyes crinkled when she smiled. She said, "I don't think you told me your name."

"It's Timothy Francis Brennan," he told her.

"And where do you live, Timothy Francis Brennan?" she went on brightly. She had a nervous, sharp way of talking.

"Duffy's Rocks," he answered, thinking he ought to add something like "ma'am," but he didn't.

"Oh," she said. "Of course. That's across the river, isn't it?" There was an almost imperceptible pause. Then she said, "Do you come often to hear the orchestra?"

Timothy was too ashamed to admit that he had never been to a real concert before, so he merely smiled back at her, hoping that she would think that he was quite used to symphony matinees.

Just then a woman she knew came up to the aisle and leaned over to speak to her. Timothy was relieved. He had been afraid she would ask him questions about classical composers and discover that he didn't know anything about them.

The last piece they played was called, according to the program, "a tone poem." For a long time it didn't sound like anything. Then Timothy relaxed and decided that it didn't matter. After that the music began to surge around him. It was like horses' hooves in his ears and waves of water and mounting flames of fire.

When it was all over Timothy and the lady filed down the aisle together. Her head was high, her eyes glowing.

"Well," she breathed. "That was simply splendid!"

Timothy nodded.

"I don't know if I thanked you for the ticket," he said. It wasn't only that he wanted to show her that he had nice manners, or that he was just doing what Gran would have wanted him to do. He felt really grateful to her. It was as though just by standing in front of the Syria Mosque a door had opened onto a world he had never known before. "I enjoyed it very much," he said.

She smiled. "I'm glad you did. It seemed a pity to have the seat go to waste. The friend with whom I usually go came down with a touch of flu at the last moment."

They were already out in the lobby. The street was just beyond them. Timothy said, smiling uncertainly and not knowing whether or not to hold out his hand, "Well, thank you again."

"Just a moment, Timothy!" she exclaimed impulsively, placing her gloved hand on his arm. "Let me give you this." She opened her blue velvet bag and found a little leather case from which she drew a small white rectangle of pasteboard. "Here," she said. "Do come and see me. I live in Shadyside. I'm in the telephone book." She pressed the card into his hand. The skin around her clear bright eyes crinkled again and the look she gave him was warm and intimate. "Good-bye, then, Timothy, for now!" She pressed his arm and was gone.

Timothy didn't look at the card until he was out in the windy street.

"Mrs. William Clyde Lachlan," he read. He ran his fingers over the surface of the letters, and the printing was bumpy to his touch. It was an engraved card. He had heard about those from Gran.

He put it carefully away in an inside pocket.

He didn't know how long the concert had taken, but the sky was already darkening, and it wasn't just because of the smoke and the soot in the air. It was getting late now. He guessed it was time to go home. Well, he told himself in the streetcar which rattled back across the river to Duffy's Rocks, he had missed the program at the Carnegie Library and when Sister Scholastica saw him on Monday she would want to know why. But it had been worth going anyway. He had gone to Pittsburgh by himself, and he had been to a real symphony concert. He didn't know how much the ticket Mrs. Lachlan had given him cost, but he was sure it was very expensive; a lot more than a movie, even a downtown movie.

And then, abruptly, he felt empty. The excitement, the memory of the music, the feeling of being rich as he sat in the soft armchair in the warm auditorium, and Mrs. Lachlan's intimate smile as she handed him her visiting card, all ebbed out of him.

The face of the man in the library reading room reemerged from the back of his mind.

He blushed at the recollection of what he had done.

He guessed that it had been a pretty loony way to behave.

Still, he told himself, the man *could* have been his father.

That night, before he went to bed, he opened the bottom dresser drawer where he kept all the mementos of his father that he possessed. He took them out and spread them on the bed.

There was a pair of leather gloves, a silk paisley scarf wrapped in tissue paper, and a little pile of photographs. There were also a few letters, no more than four or five in all.

He read the letters first.

They were all old ones, from years back, and one of them was only a postcard with a view of the Woolworth Building in New York. "Love to Timothy from his Dad," it said on the back. He tried to decipher the date on the postmark, but it was blurred. The letters were even earlier, their envelopes long since worn out and gone, and the writing on them scrawled and hasty. "Dear Timothy, thank you for your letter. I am glad to hear that you are doing well and going to my old school, St. Bridget's. I am sure the sisters there haven't changed since my time. I am writing this from Philadelphia. I may take a new job here. It is a charming old city with a great secondhand bookshop called Leary's which you must visit some day. Love from your Father." The others antedated that. He read them hungrily. Here and there a phrase jumped out at him. "I am glad that your grandmother writes me such good reports of you. . . ." "I'm in a hurry now but I will write soon again when I get a chance. . . ." "Be good to your grandmother. Maybe I'll get back to Duffy's Rocks to see you both at Christmas if I can get away. . . ."

In spite of himself, Timothy could not deny that they were noncommittal. They said nothing, really. He tried to read between the lines, to find some hidden message. There must be one, somewhere. And the Christmas he had written about had passed with no sign of him, although Timothy and Gran didn't give up waiting for him well after New Year's when they took down the holiday decorations.

Next, he turned over the photographs, studying them one by one. There was his father as a boy, with his hair falling into his eyes, holding out a baseball bat. There was his father in his class picture at college, wearing a tight suit and high starched collar. There were several from his army days, with the names of his buddies, who were also in the pictures, written on the backs. And, finally, a snapshot of him standing in a backyard. It was a backyard in some city Timothy didn't know.

There were also the books which Timothy kept on a special shelf, books which had belonged to his father. They were mostly old textbooks. The only reason Timothy treasured them was because of the name, *Bartholomew Brennan,* or *Bart Brennan,* or *B. Brennan, Esquire,* which had been written on their flyleaves in varying boyish handwritings and with dates on them from before Timothy had been born.

And that was it.

He surveyed the lot. The pair of empty gloves and the scarf in its yellowing tissue were things his father had worn. Timothy would never had dreamed of using them himself. They were his most precious possessions. But his father had left them behind with nothing of himself left in them. Timothy was sure that if he were a dog and sniffed them, they would not even hold a trace of his father's smell anymore. And the letters and the photographs weren't much more of a help. There was nothing there, no clue, nothing to tell him what his father was really like. They were no good to him. They could tell him nothing.

He put his things back in the dresser and shoved his socks over them. Then he pushed the drawer shut.

Not even Gran, he thought, had ever told what he really wanted to know. Gran had her own will about that.

No one had ever told him.

What sort of man was Bartholomew Brennan, or Bart Brennan, or B. Brennan, Esquire? Why did everyone in the family avoid talking about him?

It was like a mystery. But it was a mystery which Timothy knew he would have to solve for himself.

He opened the top drawer on his dresser and rummaged around in it until he found an old school notebook with a marble black-and-white cover. He flipped quickly through its lined pages until he came to the one he had carefully filled out earlier in the year, on New Year's morning.

He read it over.

NEW YEAR'S RESOLUTIONS
by T. F. Brennan

Today is the first day of 1934.
Today is the first day of the rest of my life.

Under that he had drawn a firm line with a ruler. Then he had gone on to write:

I will not throw spitballs in class.
I will not get on the wrong side of Sister Scholastica.
I will be debonair and kind in all my actions.
I will not get impatient with Mary Agnes.
I will be turse in speech. (The spelling looked wrong, but he decided in the end to let it stay that way.)
I will be more attentive at Mass.
I will do a kind act for my grandmother every day.
I will try to be neater in my dress and keep my shoes shined at all times.
I will save up for a pair of hunting boots with a knife in the side.
I will read at least three worthwhile and famous books every week.

Well, he hadn't kept them all, especially the one about the spitballs, but at least he had saved up a dollar and thirty-five cents toward the boots.

He thought for a moment. Then he got his pen and ink and wrote carefully across the bottom of the page:

I will find out about my father.

He added his initials and the date.

Before he shut the notebook he fished the lady's visiting card out of his pocket. He had thought of throwing it away, or of flushing it down the toilet, maybe, so that Gran wouldn't see it in the trash and ask questions. Going downtown was something which belonged to him now. What happened there was something he didn't want to share with anybody, not even Gran.

In the end he decided to keep the engraved card as a souvenir, and he tucked it inside the notebook to mark the place where he had written his resolutions.

Then he put the notebook carefully away.

He didn't open it again for a long time, but the next Saturday, on his own, he went downtown again.

TWO

The Great World
and Timothy Francis
Brennan

The first and only time that he took Mary Agnes with him on one of his Saturdays, Timothy began to regret it almost from the moment he set out.

The whole day, as a matter of fact, turned out to be a kind of disaster. And yet, in a way, it wasn't wasted. On that day the seed was planted for what Timothy was to do later.

It had not turned out at all the way that Mary Agnes had expected it to, either.

For one thing, she had known that Timothy was itching to be on his own. That only made her all the more determined to make him take her along.

It was their grandmother who settled the matter in the end.

"Ah," she snapped, "I've had enough of your wrangling. Wouldn't the walls just crack around our heads from the racket of it! Outside, now, with the both of yous. Mr. Kinsella and I will be the better for it if we're shet of yous for the day." She turned to Timothy, her pale eyes reproachful behind her rimless glasses. "As for you, Timothy Francis, I don't know where it is you find to go, all on your own, but it's not going to kill you if you take Mary Agnes with you, just once. If I know boys, you'll be on your knees to a lot worse in a few years' time, begging to do you the honor of hanging on your arm. Mary Agnes is not a person to be ashamed of."

Little did Gran know, Timothy thought bitterly while Mary Agnes performed a little wiggle of triumph behind Gran's back.

"He hates me because I'm his cousin!" Mary Agnes cried.

Gran pursed her lips. "I won't listen to such talk." Her eyes remained fixed on Timothy's sullen face. "What would your father think if I was to write him such a thing?" She beckoned him to her side. Then she reached for her worn, black, leatherette snap purse, which hung from the back of the kitchen chair. She opened it. "Here," she said quietly. "You'll be needing some extra carfare, since you have a lady along to pay for."

Timothy glanced down at his palm. There was a quarter in it. "The times is bad and the flesh is weak, so take it and use it before I change my mind," she said. "And now," she added, before he could even thank her for it, "out!"

Their grandmother's front door was less than a block behind them when, "Where are we going?" Mary Agnes demanded.

"I'm not sure yet," he told her.

Her face turned mean with suspicion.

"What do you mean you're not sure?"

The savage excitement that seized him every Saturday morning now, whenever it was time for him to go off on his expedition, had begun to boil in his veins. Grinning jauntily he said, "I never know where I'm going until I get there."

"Timothy Francis Brennan!" she exclaimed. "That's stupid."

His face clouded. It was almost a year he had been going down to Pittsburgh to explore, every Saturday. Saturdays were his own property now. They were private. Wasn't it bad enough that she had forced him to take her along this time without her deliberately trying to spoil it for him? After all, she was a big girl now, practically thirteen, only less than a year younger than he was. He couldn't see why Mary Agnes couldn't go off on adventures of her own, with her girl friends, instead of having to barge in on his personal, private arrangements.

He kicked out at a ridge of ice turned to black lace at its edge, all that was left of the snowfall of the week before. "Why is that so stupid?" he asked.

But Mary Agnes was too busy to reply. She was tugging at her long ribbed stockings. She had stopped right there on the sidewalk in front of Lesniak's grocery store to do it.

He stared disapprovingly at her until she had finished.

"Well," he persisted. "Why is it so stupid?"

Mary Agnes tried to look superior, as though those stockings were not still clinging to her thin shins in lumpy brown wrinkles.

"I always like to know where I'm going," she declared.

"Don't you like surprises?"

She pressed her lips together. "Only when I know what they're going to be," she said.

Looking at her small, set, pointed face, suspicious and already dark with disappointment, Timothy knew that it would be hopeless to explain to her that this was what he always did. He just went. And then, once he got there, he let things happen.

He called out, "Here comes the streetcar now!" and started to sprint to the car stop. Mary Agnes forgot about her stockings and panted after him. The rear door clattered open. All the seats were already taken, so they had to stand on the rear platform, holding onto the poles.

They rode in silence. Mary Agnes looked resentfully at Timothy, while Timothy looked through the soot-streaked glass. He stared at the small framed houses, all exactly like his grandmother's, with their gritty curtains stretched across the front windows. He stared at the skimpy bare trees, at the grime-layered store fronts, at the shabby beer parlors on every corner, their entrance doors clotted with unemployed men. In the center of almost every block there stood a church with its blackened brick parochial school, exactly like St. Bridget's where he and Mary Agnes went. They all flashed past as the streetcar clanged downhill.

They were like a rosary strung across the town with each bead in a different language. There was the German church, Holy Trinity; then St. Margaret of Hungary; St. Ladislaus, which was Slovak; St. Jan Nepomuk's (Czech; Mrs. Sevchick from next door went there). After that came St. Sava's, for the Serbians; the Croatian church; Sts. Cyril and Methodius, the Slovene church; the Lithuanian church with a saint's name that he couldn't pronounce; St. Josaphat's Ukrainian Catholic Church; Our Lady of Czestochowa, which was Polish; and St. Catherine of Genoa, faced all over with gaudy Italian stonework.

As the neighborhood receded, Timothy's heart bounded higher. Soon they had even left behind them Kolb's Used Car Lot where, week after week, the same automobiles stood. None of them ever seemed to get sold, in spite of the huge banners that stretched across the entrance: No Reasonable Offer Refused! Easy Terms Arranged on the Spot!

After that, the railroad tracks cut across the street. Now the faces of the unemployed men on the sidewalk were black. He looked out for the mysterious store front which had all its windows painted over in yellow and purple and red, with a sign over the doorway: AFRICAN CHURCH OF THE PENTECOSTAL BROTHERHOOD. COME TO THE REFRESHING SPRING AND BE SAVED!

Once past the church, Timothy knew that he was really on his way. There was still more than half an hour's ride ahead of him, uphill and downhill, winding through a grubby string of industrial towns exactly like Duffy's Rocks, all grown together in a shapeless suburb. Each had its rows of gaunt, gray, company houses like dingy wash on a line, and stores whose shabby windows denied the hope that prosperity was just around the corner, and more churches.

He smiled to himself now. He glanced down at his feet. He hadn't managed to save up for the boots with the knife in the side, but his old shoes shone. He had polished them himself in the kitchen the night before. His hair was combed, stiff and dark with water, and carefully parted. His white shirt crackled with starch, and although his tie was an old one, he had spent a long time getting the knot just right. His blue serge suit was shiny only where it didn't show. And if his overcoat was too small for him, that didn't matter because he could feel the money waiting in his pocket. He had his weekly dollar that he earned from carting out the ashes from Mrs. Sevchick's furnace.

He was on his way: off to the adventure that waited for him. The whole week, to him, was a trough between his Saturdays. It was the thought of them that made it possible to endure all those dreary weekdays which led up to them. For the moment he even forgot that this time Mary Agnes was with him, secured to his side like a block of cement.

Soon he would be able to see the river. Then the bulk of the skyscrapers would loom ahead of him, shining through the grit-filled air. And after that he would be downtown.

He pressed closer to the window, but just then some broad Slovak ladies got up. They clutched black oilcloth shopping bags in their chapped hands, and their faces under their shawls were steamy and red. They surrounded him, blocking the view. He could only tell when the streetcar was crossing the river from the way it lurched and from the sound of the wheels rattling on the bridge. After that the car began to empty. But there was no sense in sitting down now.

Suddenly, he grabbed Mary Agnes by the sleeve.

"Come on. We're getting off here!"

"Where?"

"Oh, come on!"

She jumped down, plunging after him into the crowds that clogged the intersection.

The great world, Timothy thought: This was it! He turned, lifting his face eagerly toward it, ignoring the people who had to jostle him in order to pass. There was not much smoke today. Everything was clear in the cold winter air. His eyes drank in the wide streets filled with traffic and lined with vast office buildings. He knew the name of every single one of the glittering granite buildings of downtown Pittsburgh. All around him, in every direction, they stretched: banks, department stores with their enormous crystal display windows, theatres. A sea of preoccupied faces milled in and out of them. Every Saturday he felt the same urge of wild exhilaration. It was all there. And it was all his!

Mary Agnes, at his shoulder, said, "What are we going to do now?"

He blinked at her. "I just like to mingle with the crowd."

It was a phrase which he especially liked that year. He had found it in a book.

Mary Agnes was not impressed by it.

"And?" she persisted.

He could have smacked her, but he only said, "And that's enough for right now. Later on, we'll see."

She trailed after him as he made his way to Smithfield Street. He walked along, oblivious of the cindery grit under his shoes, grazing hungrily into the shop windows. Even though there weren't many customers in the stores, and half the windows had big stickers pasted across them with signs like SALE, ALL PRICES SLASHED! or GOING OUT OF BUSINESS, EVERY-THING MUST BE SOLD! they were filled with wonderful objects.

"We can't buy anything," Mary Agnes said. "So what's the sense of looking?"

He said loftily, "I'm just playing my game."

She gave him a sharp, dubious look.

"What game?"

"I always play it when I'm by myself. From every window I pick the one thing I'd take."

"That's easy," she said in a decisive voice. "I'd look at the prices and then I'd just take what costs the most."

"You can't do that," he explained patiently. "It has to be something you really want for yourself. How much it costs doesn't count."

She reflected for a moment.

"Supposing it's, well, a store with nothing I could use? Then what?"

"Then you have to pick a present you would give somebody. But you have to say who it's for."

"All right. I'll take that evening bag, the one with the gold chain and the red sequins all over it."

"Who for?"

She gave him a withering look. "For myself," she said.

Slowly they proceeded up Smithfield Street. They hardly ever agreed on what they picked. Timothy was convinced that most of Mary Agnes' choices were silly, and Mary Agnes said she couldn't imagine what he would ever do with most of the things he took. Then, halfway down the other side of Smithfield, right under the Kaufmann's Department Store clock, Mary Agnes suddenly stopped.

"I don't want to look anymore," she said.

"Why not?"

"I'm cold."

He glowered at her.

"Cold?"

She chattered her teeth at him. "Yes. C.O.L.D.," she said.

"Well, that makes us even. You wanted to come, didn't you? You pestered me to come along."

"That was because you really didn't want me to. And now all we're doing is just walking around the streets looking in store windows at stuff we can't really have anyway. And I'm freezing." She sniffed. "And what are you going to do about it?"

"But we really haven't done anything yet, Mary Agnes. Come on, you'll like it. You'll see."

"I don't want to just walk around anymore. I want to go home now if we're not going to do anything warm."

Timothy stared at her. She was an infuriating sight. Her fists were crammed into the pockets of her windbreaker. Under her big, knitted green cap with its frayed white pompom her peaked gypsy face looked smaller than ever, and her lips were turning blue. Her skirt, he realized for the first time, was too short for her skinny legs. She looked angry and lost.

Then he remembered that Mary Agnes was not really used to downtown the way he was. His face softened.

He said, "Don't you like just looking at things?"

"Not when I can't have them," she retorted fiercely. "And not when I'm freezing all over."

He stood there for a moment. Then he made a sudden decision.

"All right," he said. "Come with me."

"Can't you even tell me, Timothy, where we're going?"

"You'll see in a minute."

She had to take running steps to keep up with him. And then he vanished. He had been swallowed up by the vast building in front of them. When she read the name of it she hung back, rooted to the sidewalk. She started after him in unbelief.

He waved to her through the revolving doors to follow him.

Mary Agnes refused to budge.

He had to go around again and pull her in after him.

"We can't go inside," she said in a shocked voice. "It's the William Penn Hotel!"

"Shut up, Mary Agnes!" he told her between his clenched teeth. "Who says we can't come inside?"

"But we don't know anyone here!"

"We don't have to. It's a public place, isn't it?"

She gaped at him.

"But—"

"Stop making such a fuss, Mary Agnes. Do you want people

to start looking? You said you were cold, didn't you? Well. Come on, then."

He pulled her after him across the lobby. She proceeded across the thick carpeting as though it had been woven out of eggshells.

Timothy went ahead confidently, but Mary Agnes glanced nervously at the line of bellboys with their tight uniforms and polished buttons. "They'll put us out!" she whispered.

"Not if you act like you belong here," he said sharply.

"But I don't belong here."

He ignored her.

She scooted after him past the lordly gentleman who stood behind the reception desk.

"What are you going to do now, Timothy?" she asked. Her voice shook, but it was no longer because of the cold.

"Nothing," he said firmly. "I'm just going to find a place where we can sit down."

He strode ahead of her, eyeing the bulky leather davenports that were lined up against the tall potted plants. "There's an empty one," he said.

"You can't do that!" squeaked Mary Agnes.

"Why not?" He plumped himself calmly down at one end of it. "Now you sit down too," he commanded.

Gingerly, Mary Agnes lowered herself onto it at the opposite end. The cushion slowly sank, and she sank with it.

"Don't bounce!" he warned. "Just sit there as though you were waiting for somebody."

"It's so big," she said in a loud whisper. "It's the biggest sofa I ever sat on." She giggled. "You're so far away, Timothy." She waggled her hand at him. "Yoo-hoo!" she called.

Timothy frowned.

She hastily stuffed her hand back into her pocket. Then she settled back, keeping her knees pressed closely together. "Is this all right?"

He nodded and gave her a tight smile. After that he turned to watch all the people who were moving through the warm lobby.

Mary Agnes glanced around her in awe. Two ladies in fur coats and feathered hats were talking animatedly on the sofa across from theirs. One of the ladies held a little dog on her lap. The dog had on a red woollen sweater.

After a moment Marry Agnes said, "You want to know something, Timothy?"

"What?"

"You look different."

"How, different?"

"I don't know." She considered. "You look almost like somebody who was staying here, like some rich kid from out of town." She giggled again. "I can't help it," she said. "If all those people at the desk knew, they'd throw us right out of here and chase us home."

He glanced at her with annoyance. "They wouldn't do any such thing," he said firmly. All the same, his eyes flickered in the direction of the gods at the reception desk, just to be sure.

Mary Agnes' eyes wandered cautiously around the lobby, taking in the groups of chatting ladies, the men in felt hats and heavy overcoats dashing off to important appointments, the porters pushing their way behind carts piled with sumptuous luggage, the small whirlpool of activity around the elevator doors. The cigar counter was not far from where they sat. "You don't even have to go outside to buy a newspaper!" she exclaimed.

"I bet there are people here from every single city in the world," Timothy told her.

She sighed. "I wonder," she said, curling her warm toes, "what it would be like, sleeping in a hotel like this?"

He did not answer. He had been thinking the same thing, and deciding that one day he would find out for himself. He would know when his father would send for him. Hotels like this were nothing special to Bart Brennan. The letters Gran got from him, which were a little more frequent than those which Timothy received, were almost always on thick hotel stationery from some big city or other. There hadn't been any for a long time, but that, as Gran had explained, was because his father had been much too busy lately to write.

"How much do you think it costs?" Mary Agnes was asking. "You know: room and board?"

He surveyed the lobby possessively. "Plenty," he said.

"Like five dollars? A day, I mean?"

"Even more, maybe."

She sank back against the davenport, breathless, and let herself drown in comfort. She was thinking. Once her hand stole out, when Timothy wasn't looking, to stroke the green tree that grew out of the porcelain jar on the floor next to the davenport. It was real.

At last she turned to Timothy.

"Can't you tell me now," she pleaded, "what you really do when you come downtown? I know you don't spend the whole day walking around. If you tell me, Timothy, I won't tell a single solitary soul, not even Gran."

"I don't care if you tell her," he said. "I just go to different places, that's all."

"Like where?" She leaned forward, licking her lips. "Like the movies?"

"Sometimes. But the movies aren't all that special. You don't have to come downtown for that." He paused. Then he said, "I went to a symphony concert once."

"Timothy, you didn't!"

"I was standing outside watching the people go in, and a lady gave me a ticket."

"You mean she just gave it to you, like that?"

"She said she had an extra one. It was right down in the orchestra."

"Honestly!" Mary Agnes' eyes glittered. "How was it, Timothy? It must have been terribly loud." Before he could answer, she went on, "I don't know if I'd have cared so much for it, listening to all that classical music. I mean, all those notes, and it never seems to go anywhere, does it? I'd have liked it better if it was a movie. Still, it was free, wasn't it?"

It had been a lot of notes, Timothy reflected. But how was he to explain to her what it was like, sitting in the hushed atmosphere of the Syria Mosque with everyone around him in their best clothes, and the seat he sat in soft and comfortable, and the music surging around him?

"What else?"

"Well, I go to Schenley Park sometimes, but it's too cold for that now. And sometimes I go to the Institute."

"That's a museum, like, isn't it? What can you do there?"

"I look around. It has paintings."

Mary Agnes reflected. Then, "That's too much like church,"

she decided. She slid over closer to him and squinted into his face. "What else do you do?"

"Oh," he told her, "I just go around, like I said." He paused. "And I have lunch."

"Where, Timothy? In the cafeteria?"

He looked scornful. "No," he said. "In a restaurant."

"One with real waiters?"

"Of course."

"Honestly!" Mary Agnes exclaimed again. She thought about it for a moment. "Don't you get embarrassed?"

"No. Why should I?"

"I would, if I was to go all by myself."

"There's nothing to it," he assured her. He glanced up at the bronze clock over the bank of elevators. Its hands already pointed at one. He felt in his pocket. The money was still there.

He turned to Mary Agnes.

"Are you hungry?"

"Not specially," she said, but her tongue stole out furtively and traveled across her upper lip.

"I'll tell you what," he said, breaking into a smile. "We'll eat in a restaurant today. I'll take you."

"Do you mean that, Timothy? Really?" Her face was suffused with excitement. Then it fell. "I only have fifteen cents. It's all I saved this week."

"I'll treat you, Mary Agnes," he told her expansively.

She scanned his face.

"If I say I will, I will," he said.

"I only mean," she told him humbly, "are you sure you have enough money, Timothy?"

That's my business." He grinned at her. "All right," he said. "Are you ready to go now?"

She nodded.

"Then come on. And no more being cold."

"I won't say a word, I promise, even if my nose freezes! Anyway," she added, scurrying after him toward the revolving doors, "it was getting terribly hot in here."

Out on the windy sidewalk, the two ladies with a dog were getting into the automobile.

"Well," said Mary Agnes, in a patronizing voice, loud enough for them to hear, "I think it's a very nice little hotel, considering." Then she raced down the street after Timothy.

They went on in silence, not bothering to stop in front of windows anymore. But then, on one corner, there was a store with an enormous expanse of polished stone façade in which were set three tiny display windows. They were lit up like miniature theatres.

"We have to look in here!" Mary Agnes said. She pressed her forehead against the cold pane. "Ooh," she cried. "Look, Timothy. It's all gold and diamonds."

"What did you expect? It's a jewelry store."

"Let's choose something."

Their eyes raked the display.

Timothy joggled her elbow. "How about the necklace?"

"Do you think all those diamonds and rubies could be real?"

"Of course they are."

Her mouth curved in disdain. "Well, I think it's awfully gaudy."

"Gaudy? It must be worth thousands and thousands of dollars!"

"I don't care. I'd never wear anything like that. It looks like glass."

They abandoned the diamond-and-ruby necklace and moved on to the second window. It was lined with white satin, against which had been arranged three gold cigarette cases. "Wouldn't you think they'd have more to show than that?" Mary Agnes remarked contemptuously as she tugged at her stockings.

The last window held crystal and silver tableware.

Mary Agnes let out a little gasp. In the center of the display stood a tiny silver vase with a single rose in it.

Timothy had seen it at the same time.

They stared at it.

"I wonder how much something like that costs?" Mary Agnes said at last.

"We can find out."

Her jaw went slack. "Timothy Francis Brennan, you wouldn't have the nerve to walk in there and ask them. Never!"

"Wouldn't I?"

She shook her head.

"Then you just stand there and watch me."

He moved toward the massive, bronze-barred door.

"Timothy!" she wailed. "Come back! You'll get arrested!"

He disregarded her and went inside. After a while she saw a man's manicured hand reach into the window through the little curtain behind it and remove the vase. A few minutes later the same hand carefully replaced it. And then Timothy was out there on the street beside her.

Mary Agnes' eyes were as big and as round as coat buttons. "Did they really let you hold it?"

He nodded.

"And? Well, what did they say?"

"They said it cost fifteen dollars. It's sterling silver. And they called me *sir*."

"Honestly!"

"And if I had fifteen dollars," he added, as they charged across the street before the green light changed, "I would have bought it."

"I bet you would too, Timothy!" Mary Agnes' eyes were swimmy with admiration.

He only smiled.

When they reached the opposite curb, he had an idea. "I know a short cut to the restaurant," he said.

"All right. Anything you say, Timothy."

"It's nothing great. We can just walk through Gimbels and out the other side. That way you won't be so cold."

"Cold!" She sniffed. "Who's cold? And we can go down in the basement. That's where Mama shops."

They made slow progress through Gimbel's basement because there were so many things which she had to stop and finger, and every other minute she had to run on so as not to lose Timothy. One of the very last counters had a little sign: Genuine Mosaic Brooches Imported from Florence, Italy. It was Timothy who lingered to inspect them.

"What do you think of that?" he said. "Look, Mary Agnes. They're all made of little bits of colored glass stuck together."

"They look like flowers!"

Together they pored over them. "I like the one you're holding," Mary Agnes said.

"Wouldn't it be nice for Gran, though!"

The big blonde lady behind the counter leaned over toward them. "Pretty, aren't they?" she remarked. "They're a special. And a real bargain, too. Only fifty-nine cents."

They stared at her. Mary Agnes was fascinated by her red earrings and bleached hair.

The saleslady's red fingernails plucked the brooch from Timothy's hand and held it against her blouse. "This one's very classy. Forget-me-nots it's supposed to be. It would make a very gorgeous present for somebody."

Timothy wavered.

The saleslady flashed a smile at him. "I could wrap it for you real nice," she said. "In a gift box with a lining."

"Timothy!" Mary Agnes exclaimed. "You're not going to buy it!"

"Why not?" he said grandly. "It would look nice on Gran." He hauled some money out of his pocket. "I'll take it," he told the saleslady.

"You picked the best one," she assured him. "You got lovely taste."

"He's my cousin," Mary Agnes told her.

When they left the counter the forget-me-not brooch was nested in yellow cotton inside a little box which had "Made in Italy" stamped on the cover.

"Can't you just see Gran's face when she opens it!" said Mary Agnes. "She'll die!"

A few yards away something else drew Mary Agnes' eye. "Hey, Timothy. Look at this!" A small, brown, burlap object dangled from her hand.

"What's that?"

"It's supposed to be a catnip mouse. Anyway, that's what it says on the label."

"I bet Mr. Kinsella would like that," he said.

She looked dubious. "Mr. Kinsella's too old."

Timothy looked at the price tag. "It's only a nickel, marked down from nineteen cents. I'll get it. We can see what Mr. Kinsella does with it."

Mary Agnes cast her eyes quickly around her. Then she lowered her voice. "You go on ahead. I'll hook it."

"What are you talking about, Mary Agnes?"

"Ah, it's easy. Nobody's looking."

"Are you crazy? Here, in Gimbels? They have detectives all over the place."

He fished out a nickel and paid for it. Then, with the pin for their grandmother and the mouse for Mr. Kinsella safely stuffed into his overcoat pocket, they floated up to the main floor on the escalator and made their way out onto the street.

"All the same," said Mary Agnes, "if I hadn't said anything to you I could have swiped it easy."

They walked briskly now. Timothy was hungry. He had been too excited at the prospect of going downtown to eat much breakfast, and now he found himself wishing he hadn't spurned the bowl of oatmeal Gran had set down for him. "It's only a few blocks from here, where we're going," he announced. Mary Agnes didn't mind how far it was. Her eyes were bright, and she didn't seem to feel the cold anymore.

And then, around the corner, there it was.

"Is *that* the place?" she asked.

"It doesn't look like what I imagined. 'MARIO'S CONTINENTALE. ITALIAN AND FRENCH CUISINE,'" she read aloud from the sign across the front of it. She wrinkled her nose. "It's foreign," she said.

"But that's the whole point!"

The menu, mimeographed in runny purple ink, was stuck on the inside of the window. "See?" Timothy said. "'Special five-course table d'hôte luncheon, 45¢, glass of wine included.'"

"Wine?" she said, scandalized. "Honestly!" She bent to read

the menu. "'Choice of entree.' . . . It's all French and Italian. How do you know what to order?"

"If you don't know, you just ask the waiter and he explains what it is."

"And show him I don't know? I'd never!"

"Oh, come on, Mary Agnes. I'm starving. You can have spaghetti. You like that, don't you?"

"Only when it's out of a can." She pressed her face against the steamy glass and peered through it at the tables set with red-checked cloths and baskets of breadsticks.

"Oh, all right," she agreed. "But I'm not drinking any of that wine!"

Timothy started to sail ahead of her through the door. Then, suddenly, he stopped. He pulled his money out of his pockets and began to count it.

"What's the matter?" Mary Agnes asked.

He looked up at her in dismay. "I didn't think about it when I bought the pin for Gran. We don't have enough."

"Not even with my fifteen cents?"

He calculated. Then he shook his head. "There's the tip, too. You have to leave a dime each."

"Couldn't we just get up when the waiter wasn't looking and walk away very quickly?"

"No," he said. "Anyway, even without the tip there's nothing left."

Mary Agnes had an inspiration. "Look, we could just order one lunch. You could eat half and I'd eat the rest."

He shook his head impatiently. "They don't let you do that."

She reflected. "Maybe they'd take the pin back at Gimbels. We could say it wasn't the right color or something. Mama's always doing that."

Timothy thought about it.

"I don't think the saleslady would mind," Mary Agnes put in. "She looked real kind."

"No," Timothy said at last. "I wouldn't like to disappoint Gran."

"But if she doesn't know we bought it for her, how can she be disappointed?"

"I wouldn't feel right taking it back once we bought it for her," he said slowly.

The door of Mario's Continentale swung open. Two men walked out, releasing a hot whiff of food from the restaurant. Timothy and Mary Agnes looked at the people inside, sitting at the little tables, working their way through the five-course table d'hôte.

"Well, Timothy, what are we going to do?"

"We can't just stand here," he said.

She tugged at his arm. "Let's go," she said.

"I'm sorry for your disappointment, Mary Agnes," he said, swallowing his own.

"It doesn't matter, really," she lied. "I'm glad we got the pin for Gran."

Reluctantly, they moved away.

"We'll have to eat something," Timothy told her.

"Don't worry, we'll find a place," she said. "How much do we have left?"

He counted it all again.

"Sixty-eight cents, but that's counting your fifteen and what we have to leave out for carfare home."

"Oh, we're rich!" she said. "Let's start looking."

In the end they settled for Woolworth's. Baked beans were ten cents at the lunch counter.

"They're very filling," Timothy admitted. "But the hot franks are only ten cents too, and you can pile on all the mustard and relish you want."

So they had the frankfurters, and on the way out they paused at the candy department. Peanut brittle was twenty-seven cents a pound.

"We can afford a whole pound," Mary Agnes announced, "and we'll still have enough left over for carfare and a penny change."

Then they were out on the streets again, munching as they passed the bag of peanut brittle back and forth between them. "I like the pecan crunch better, but it costs more," Mary Agnes said, with her mouth full.

They walked without any plan. They stood outside all the movie theatres, inspecting the still photographs in the outer lobbies. "I wish I had a name like Merle Oberon or Miriam Hopkins," Mary Agnes said dreamily as she scanned the display of Coming Attractions, "instead of"—she made a face—"Mary Agnes Doyle."

"There's nothing to stop you from calling yourself Merle or Miriam if you wanted."

She smiled at the thought. The next moment her rapturous expression turned into a sour grimace.

"I'd never. They'd all laugh. Can't you just hear Uncle Matt and Aunt Anna when I told them to call me Merle? And Gran?"

Timothy remembered his grandmother's mocking laughter the day he had announced he was going to call himself T. Frank Brennan.

"Maybe you're right," he said slowly. Then he thought about being an actor. You could be anybody you wanted to be, then. You could be a thousand different people. Aloud, he said, "Of course if you were an actor nobody could say anything about it if you changed your name. They do it all the time."

"I wouldn't want to be an actress," Mary Agnes said. "There's all that kissing they have to do. I wonder how they manage. Don't their teeth ever get in the way?"

The bright theatre façade faded behind them as they moved off.

"I wonder what time it is?" Timothy said. He looked around until he found a clock in a bank window. "I guess we ought to be heading back."

"All right, Timothy," she said in a quiet voice. "There isn't anything else to see. We've seen just about everything there is, haven't we? And anyway, my feet are starting to hurt."

Timothy's feet were tired too, but he didn't say so.

A hard wind rose. It whipped at their legs as they stood on the corner waiting for a streetcar.

"I'm sorry about the lunch, Mary Agnes," he said.

"Oh, ish-kabibble!"

The streetcar came rushing toward them. They climbed in, found seats, and settled themselves.

Mary Agnes pressed his arm.

"You want to know something, Timothy?"

"What?"

"I think you can do anything," she said. Her dark pointed face shone with admiration. "Just anything!"

But Timothy was not really listening to her. His gazed was fixed on the tall buildings of downtown, brilliant in the sharp light of the sinking winter sun, as he prepared himself for the long ride home.

THREE

A Cold House

C rossing the river, winding, climbing the shabby valley side, descending again and climbing once more, the trolley made its way back to Duffy's Rocks.

Mary Agnes sat quietly beside him, while Timothy looked listlessly out of the window. A gray twilight had begun to spread over everything by now; night came early at this time of year.

As they drew closer to home a sinking feeling came over him. He hated Duffy's Rocks. He hated the Works with its stacks that belched its perpetual grime over everything. He hated the streets with the lusterless stores and flimsy houses. He thought with a brief glimmer of hope that perhaps today the letter would have come. He had been waiting for it for so long now: the letter from his father, saying that he was coming to get him and take him away to some city in the East, New York maybe, where everything was different, where he would live in the great world of a glorious downtown. He would go to a real high school, like the ones he read about in books, instead of dreary St. Bridget's with its little nuns who didn't teach you the things you wanted to learn and who had no idea of what the real world was like. How could they?

But even as he hoped for it, Timothy knew that the letter wouldn't have come. As Gran kept telling him, times were hard . . . It wasn't easy for his father . . . He would have to be patient.

He sighed. It wasn't easy, being patient. He had been patient ever since he could remember.

They got to their stop at last. He and Mary Agnes got out and trudged up the street to the house.

He glanced at the curtains in the front room. It didn't matter that there was no light behind them—Gran often sat in the half dark in the afternoons to save electricity. But the curtains usually stirred, almost imperceptibly, to indicate that Gran had been watching for him. There was no movement this time. Gran didn't open the door for them either. There was no sign of her. He was fumbling for the front door key when Mary Agnes, trying the door, exclaimed, "It's not locked!"

They pushed inside. Mr. Kinsella ran toward them and mewed, rubbing against their legs in the empty hall.

Timothy pulled the bags with the presents out of his coat pockets and set them on the hall table. There was no letter for him on it.

The house was strangely chilly. Timothy frowned. He had shaken down the kitchen range the first thing in the morning, shoveled out the ashes and put fresh coal on the fire. All Gran had to do was put more coal on it later from the scuttle he had filled and placed nearby. Gran never let the fire go out.

"Gran!" he called. There was no answer.

"She couldn't have gone out," Mary Agnes said. "There's her coat, hanging up. Anyway, she'd have waited for us."

"Isn't Aunt Loretta home yet?"

"Mama said she'd be a little late. She had to shop for food."

The kitchen was tidy and empty and as chilly as the rest of the house. There was nothing on the stove. Even Gran's kettle was cold.

"Gran!" he called again.

Mr. Kinsella, who had trailed after him, mewed and bounded out to the stairs. Then he ran up the landing, where he mewed again and waited.

Mary Agnes wandered upstairs after the cat.

"Timothy!" she called suddenly in a queer, squeaky voice. "Come up here right away."

He raced up to the second floor. Mary Agnes stood in the doorway of Gran's bedroom, a peculiar expression on her face.

Gran was lying on the bed, in all her clothes. She hadn't even taken her shoes off. They loomed black and large on the clean white counterpane, as though they weren't really a part of her.

Timothy pushed into the room, Mary Agnes behind him.

"Gran!" he called. "Are you all right, Gran?" He had never known his grandmother to lie down in the middle of the day.

Mr. Kinsella leaped onto the bed and settled beside her, his great yellow eyes blinking at them.

"She looks funny," Mary Agnes whispered.

He had never seen his grandmother look like that. She lay with her face turned toward the ceiling, her eyes open, and her glasses slightly askew on her ashy face. Her mouth was slightly open, and her thin lips had turned a queer bluish color against which her dentures shone with unaccustomed whiteness. Her hands clutched the counterpane, the veins in them standing out in knots, and her fingernails were the same unnatural color as her lips.

"Gran!" Timothy said. He bent over her.

She was breathing.

Her mouth twitched.

"Is it you, Tim?" she said at last. He had to strain to hear her.

"I'm here, Gran. Mary Agnes is with me. What's the matter, Gran? Don't you feel well?"

"I don't know what happened," she whispered, without moving her head. "I lay down, and then I—" Then she focused her eyes on him. "I'll be all right," she said, with an effort.

"Can't I do something for you, Gran?"

"Tell Mary Agnes to get me a good strong cup of hot tea. Then go to the store and call the doctor. You'll have to call his house. Take a nickel from my bag if you need it." Her voice seemed to be coming from somewhere beyond her.

He looked around wildly.

"Her bag's under the pillow," Mary Agnes said.

He opened it. He fumbled through the purse. There was no change in it, so he took a crumpled dollar bill.

"You take care of her until I get back, Mary Agnes," he said as he ran outside. "I'll send Mrs. Sevchick over."

Mrs. Sevchick, next door, did not answer when he banged on her porch window. He waited, banged again, and peered through the pane. Mrs. Sevchick wasn't home.

He raced down to the corner to Lesniak's store.

Mrs. Lesniak, fat and red-faced, stood behind the counter in her shapeless sweater.

"What can I get for you today, Timmy?" she asked cheerfully.

"Can you change me a dollar bill? I have to make a telephone call."

"Call?" she said. "You can't call. The telephone ain't working. They was supposed to come yesterday to fix it. I ain't seen no sign of them yet. Try the drugstore."

Both phone booths at the drugstore were occupied. Timothy shifted from foot to foot as he waited, but there was no sign of either conversation ending.

Gran looked bad, he thought. He had never seen her like that. And she hardly ever sent for the doctor for herself.

The people in the booths were still gabbing away. They were settled in forever, it looked like, both of them.

Why did Gran have to get sick on a Saturday afternoon when the doctor's office in Duffy's Rocks was closed? He knew well enough where he lived. It was on Squirrel Hill. Timothy would have to cross the river again. It would take twenty minutes at least to get there. Supposing he took a taxi? After all, he had Gran's dollar. He went outside. There was no taxi in sight. What would a taxi ever come to Duffy's Rocks for? However, the streetcar was coming that went in the direction of Squirrel Hill. He dashed across the street and leaped onto it.

It was dark now: not just the usual dark from the Works' chimneys. Night had fallen already.

He was too restless to sit down in the streetcar. He stood on the rear platform, thinking about the doctor. Why did Gran have to send him to Dr. Rosenberg, when Dr. Giltrap lived only three blocks away? But Gran didn't believe in Dr. Giltrap. She always said she wouldn't trust him to mend her shoes, and whenever anyone asked her why she didn't go to him, her face always took on a distant mocking expression. He remembered the time when Mrs. Goggin came over to see her and announced that her grandson, Terence, was studying to be a doctor. Gran had looked at Mrs. Goggin in dreadful misbelief. She knew that it would only be a terrible waste of time and money. Gran was positive that only a Jewish doctor, like Dr. Rosenberg, had the touch.

As the trolley rattled along to Squirrel Hill, Timothy began to feel nervous. He had never been there after dark. He knew that only Jews lived in the Squirrel Hill section. The other boys at St. Bridget's had filled his ears with stories about them that would make your insides curdle. They said that if the Jewish kids caught you in their neighborhood they cut you, and then you were marked forever like them. They ate strange things, too, like—well, no one was terribly sure what; and if they so much as touched a piece of ham or bacon to their lips, their tongues shriveled. And Jews couldn't work on Saturdays. That was part of their religion. In alarm, Timothy thought, suppose Dr. Rosenberg refused to come and see Gran because it was Saturday, and Gran died?

He peered out at the night-shrouded streets. They were all tree-lined, with lawns and bushes. The houses weren't stuck together like the ones in Duffy's Rocks, but set apart, each with its own garage. That was the worst of it: you never knew who might be lurking in the bushes or behind those garages.

When he jumped off the trolley, he glanced around him with apprehension. So far as he could make out, there was no one laying for him in the bushes. All the same, he kept to the lighted part of the sidewalk, half expecting a gang of boys, armed with glittering butcher knives, to come after him at every step.

But no one appeared.

Panting and safe he reached the house. It was red brick, like all the others on that block, with Tudor trim and tiny windows set in metal frames which swung outwards. The only distinguishing mark on it was the opaque glass plaque in the front window with black lettering on it: Maxwell Rosenberg, M.D. From behind the cream-colored blinds, all evenly pulled down in a way that Gran would have approved of, came the warm glow of lamplight.

He took a breath, ran up the steps to the porch, and rang the bell.

After a few minutes a maid came to the door.

"Yes? Who is it?"

"I have to see Dr. Rosenberg. Is he home?"

"He's sitting down to his supper now. This isn't his office. He don't receive patients at home."

"It's an emergency."

"Well, let me ask him if he can see anybody. Come in here and wait." She pointed through the entrance archway to the living room and disappeared.

He walked carefully across the carpet and sat down. There were magazines on a table, but he didn't pick one up. The room looked different from the waiting room of his office in Duffy's Rocks. There was a warm smell of dinner from the back of the house. It didn't smell any different from anybody else's dinner. And the room itself: he wondered how anyone could tell that it was Jewish, just from looking at it. It had just the kind of furniture anybody would buy who had the money to go to a good store downtown.

He folded his hands and waited. A grandfather clock ticked away noisily in the corner.

Then Dr. Rosenberg was standing in the doorway in his vest and shirtsleeves, wiping his sandy moustache with a napkin. He was a heavy-set man with a bald spot and dark eyes, over which hung heavy eyebrows.

"I know who you are," he said. "Let me think a minute. Of course, you're Mrs. Brennan's grandson. Well, what's wrong with you?"

"Nothing's wrong with me, Doctor. It's my grandmother. She's sick. She sent me to get you." Then he broke off. It wasn't only Dr. Rosenberg's dinnertime. It was also Saturday. He had heard that Jews wouldn't even drive their cars on Saturday.

Dr. Rosenberg looked at him and sucked gravely on a tooth. "Well," he said, "we can't let anything happen to Mrs. Brennan." He smiled. "She's a great woman, your grandmother. I'll get my bag. Wait here. My car's out in front of the house."

In a moment he was back, wearing his jacket. "I won't be long," he called out to someone in the depths of the house. In the hall he collected his coat, his hat, his scarf, and his gloves. Then he motioned to Timothy to open the front door.

In the car, Dr. Rosenberg didn't say much. He asked Timothy a few questions about the way Gran had looked, nodded when Timothy told him, and then settled back and concentrated on driving.

Timothy kept stealing glances at Dr. Rosenberg. He tried to imagine what it would be like to live in a house like the doctor's. Then he found himself wondering how it would feel to be Dr. Rosenberg's son. He knew that the doctor had children—he had seen photographs of them on the wall in his office, under the framed medical school Latin diplomas. If Dr. Rosenberg were his father, they would have long talks about all those books in Rosenbergs' living room, and sometimes they would sit down and hold serious discussions about Timothy's future. With a father like Dr. Rosenberg, he decided, it wouldn't even matter so much about being Jewish. . . . Then he thought guiltily that it was wrong, surely, to be thinking such thoughts with Gran sick, dying maybe.

It didn't take them long to reach Duffy's Rocks.

After Dr. Rosenberg's home, Timothy felt a little ashamed of Gran's house, and the dingy, run-down neighborhood.

But the doctor didn't seem to notice the bareness of everything.

Mary Agnes opened the door for them.

"Is that the doctor?" Aunt Loretta called down from Gran's room.

"I'll go up," Dr. Rosenberg said. Without bothering to take off his coat and hat, he charged up the stairs.

"How's Gran now?" Timothy asked Mary Agnes.

"The same, I guess," she said. "Mama came home just after you left. Gran drank the tea I made her, though. I think it did her good."

The house, Timothy noticed, felt less bleak. The chill had left it.

"I fixed the stove," Mary Agnes explained. "It wasn't hard. There was just enough fire left for the coal to catch on."

Timothy hung up his coat carefully, just as though Gran were downstairs to make sure he did.

"I could get you some peanut butter and crackers or something," Mary Agnes said.

"I'm not hungry," he lied.

He lowered himself down onto the edge of the sofa. It seemed hard and uncomfortable after the deep armchair in Dr. Rosenberg's house. Then his eyes fell on Gran's empty chair and he turned his gaze away from it once, ashamed of his disloyalty in comparing Gran's house with the one in

Squirrel Hill. He looked around at Gran's parlor. Everything in it was neat and spare, and everything had the air of being a little worn out with the effort of remaining neat and decent in that grimy street. His eyes fell on the ugly fireplace, faced with gleaming bile-colored tiles, with its place for a gas heater that they never used. Then his gaze traveled to the white window curtains that she washed every week, and it seemed to him that he could hear her repeating, "No dirty lace curtains for us, I'll have you know. Just clean, starched muslin, thank you."

He remembered her stories about the grand house in Oakland, where she had worked as a parlormaid when she first came over, green as a blade of grass, from Liverpool. Mrs. Tyson had died before Timothy was born, but until she died, Gran had gone once a month to visit the old lady. And it was from Mrs. Tyson's mansion that she had been married. That was where she had learned how things had to be done, and how they had to be kept up.

After she was married (she had told him this many a time), every day when his grandfather came home from the Works she made him wash; and not just his hands and face like all the other husbands in Duffy's Rocks. She had a tub all ready in the kitchen, and he had to strip to the waist and sponge himself with soap and hot water. After that she gave him his dinner.

It wasn't in the kitchen that they ate, either, like everybody else in Duffy's Rocks. It was in the dining room, at a properly spread table with a cloth and cut-glass pickle dishes and all. "And if any of my neighbors dared to criticize me for my ways, I would tell them, 'We're not bog Irish, I'll have you know, but Liverpool Irish!'"

Mr. Kinsella, routed by the doctor's visit, came downstairs and settled in front of the kitchen range, one foot sticking stiffly in the air, and set to washing his belly. Mary Agnes stared straight ahead of her, rubbing one shoe against the other. Her lips were moving. He knew she was saying a Hail Mary for Gran.

He wanted to say one too. He knew that it was what he should be doing, but he couldn't. He just sat there listening to the sounds from upstairs. All he could hear was an occasional creaking footstep from Gran's room.

He was too restless to sit there any longer, thinking about Gran, remembering things about her as though she was dead. He got up.

As he did so, his eyes fell on the framed printed lines, all wreathed in shamrocks, that hung near the door. They had always hung there. He knew by heart what they said:

May the road rise to meet you. May the wind be always at your back. May the sun shine warm upon your face, the rains fall soft upon your fields and, until we meet again, may God hold you in the palm of His hand.

And, underneath, it said, "An Irish Blessing."

He said that under his breath instead of a Hail Mary.

Then Dr. Rosenberg came downstairs with Aunt Loretta.

"She'll be all right," he heard the doctor saying in his quiet re-assuring voice. "I had to tell her, 'Let *me* give the diagnosis. You just tell me how you feel!'" He chuckled at the recollection. "It's nothing serious," he went on. "She needed some rest and a little quiet. And no housework. This house is too much for her."

"It's hers," Aunt Loretta said. "She'll never leave it."

"Well, don't worry about her, don't let her worry about herself, and make sure she doesn't do too much, no matter what she says."

"Should she take anything? Medicine, I mean?"

"You could maybe send the boy over to the drugstore for— No, I have some here in my bag. It's only drops to keep her heart quiet. Just do what it says on the bottle."

Timothy saw Aunt Loretta hold something out to the doctor as they stood inside the door.

"What's that?" Dr. Rosenberg asked.

"Just something on account, Doctor."

He shoved her hand away. "We'll talk about that some other time," he said.

"Well, good night, Doctor. Thanks a million for coming. On a Saturday night, too!"

"For your mother, I'd even come on a Sunday," he said. He laughed. "Mrs. Brennan has a wicked tongue," he told her as he went out, "but thank God she has a good heart and a strong one."

Aunt Loretta shut the door behind him. She let out a long whistle and ran her hands through her bright black hair. "Anyone seen my bag? I'll drop dead unless I have a cigarette."

"It's in the kitchen, Mama. I'll get it," Mary Agnes said quickly.

Aunt Loretta flopped onto the couch.

"I have problems enough," she said, "without Herself getting sick!"

She looked tired, Timothy thought. Her Kelly-green dress looked too bright, her fake jewelry too shiny. The seams of her silk stockings were a little crooked—but then they always were—and her red pumps, scuffed and run down at the heels, lay on the floor where she had kicked them off.

"Can I go and see her?" Timothy asked.

Aunt Loretta was rubbing the back of her neck with both her thumbs. "It always gets me right here," she said. "I guess it's all right for you to go up, but for God's sake, don't stay too long."

Mary Agnes came back into the room with her mother's bag.

"I'll go up with you," she said.

Aunt Loretta took the bag from her, rooted around in it until she produced a crumpled pack of Luckies, pulled one out, and lit it.

"You will not," she said. "You'll stay down here and give me a hand in the kitchen. I've got to fix supper and carry something upstairs for your grandmother; and I can tell you straight from the horse's mouth I don't feel like it after that day I had on the job. Everybody beefing, all day long. That's the worst of it with those people on the Project. You'd think they'd be grateful to be getting a check every week, but no!" She blew out a cloud of smoke. "And somebody has to feed that cat."

"Don't worry, I'll help you," Mary Agnes said. "I always do, don't I?" She went on eagerly, "Ma!"

"What?"

"Do you know what Tim and I did today?"

"You went off and left your grandmother alone in a freezing house, that's what you did."

"Ah, Ma!"

Aunt Loretta closed her eyes for a moment and inhaled the smoke from her cigarette. "You can tell me tomorrow on the way to church. I have a date after supper and I don't know when I'll find the time to touch up my hair. It's already beginning to show at the roots." She opened her eyes and inspected the red enamel on her fingernails. "They're all chipped, every single one of them! I figured on doing them at the office, but you can't get anything done in that loony bin. And," she added accusingly, "my bottle of nail polish just happens to have disappeared."

"I didn't touch it! I swear!"

"It just became lost," Aunt Loretta muttered.

After a pause, "Is it Mr. Constantino?" Mary Agnes asked.

"Uh huh. None other."

Mary Agnes made a face.

"And what's wrong, I want to know, with my going out sometimes with Mr. Patsy Constantino?" Aunt Loretta lashed out. "He's my boss. I wouldn't even have that job on the Sewing Project if it wasn't for him."

"He's Italian."

"Well," Aunt Loretta snapped. "They're Catholics, aren't they?"

Mary Agnes, wrinkling her nose, observed, "They're greasy!"

"Mr. Constantino is not a bit 'greasy,' as you say. He wears nice clothes. And he always uses after-shave."

"Pee-yoo!" Mary Agnes held her nose. "I hate men who use after-shave."

"When was the last time you went out with one?"

Mary Agnes refused to be quelled. "Gran says she'd rather see you going out with a Protestant any time than with an Italian."

Aunt Loretta laughed, showing her white teeth with their pointed canines.

"Herself and her ideas! They're all right for Liverpool in Queen Victoria's time. But we're living in modern times and the U.S. of A.!"

Timothy quietly took the bag with Gran's present from the hall table and went upstairs.

He pushed Gran's door open. The light was on. She was lying on the bed, under the covers. She was out of her clothes now and in her nightgown. Her hair lay flat on the pillow in a neat, thin, gray braid. Her lips were no longer that ghastly blue, but her face was still as white as paper.

He stood there in the doorway listening to her breathing. He couldn't be sure whether she was awake or not.

And then she spoke to him.

"Bart," he heard her say. "It's you. So you're back."

He strode across the mottled brown linoleum and went to her side.

"It's me, Gran," he said, looking down at her. "Timothy."

She gave him a thin smile. "Oh, so it is. For a minute I thought you was your father. He was always a fine doorful of a man. He was like your grandfather in that."

The boy glanced across the room to the photograph which stood on her bare dresser top, along with her brush and comb and her hand mirror. He was a stocky, broad-shouldered soldier in puttees staring into the camera with an engaging, light-hearted grin. If only he could be like that, he thought. But he would never.

He took her hand. He noticed for the first time how loosely the plain gold wedding band encircled her finger. "How are you feeling, Gran?" he asked.

Her lips twisted with a flash of mockery.

"The Devil wouldn't have me yet, Tim."

"Oh, Gran," he said. "Don't talk like that."

"My work isn't over. I still have to get you to college."

He fished in the Gimbels bag and drew out the little gift box.

"Here, Gran," he said. "I bought you something from downtown."

She looked at the box and then at him.

"Go on," he urged, pushing it toward her. "Open it."

"You open it for me," she said. "It'll be more of a present that way."

Timothy lifted the lid, revealing the mosaic forget-me-nots in their nest of cotton. "It's a brooch," he said. He added hastily, "It was on sale."

"Oh, it's too fine for an old woman like me," she said, her eyes resting on it with satisfaction. "Save it for your sweetheart."

"Ah Gran, it's for you! Do you like it? Put it on. Let's see it on you."

"I ought to wear it to church first."

"Just try it now. You can put it on again when you go to church."

"I can't pin a rich-looking thing like that on my old nightgown!"

"Why not? If you're sick you might as well look nice." He pinned it on her. "There. How does that look?"

"It looks just grand, I'm sure," she said. She peered at it. "Mrs. Tyson that I used to work for had one just like it. She brought it back when they went to Europe once. It ended up with the married daughter."

"You see, Gran?"

She suddenly pressed her lips together and let her head sink back on the pillow.

"Are you sure you're all right, Gran?"

She said with an effort, "I'm just a little tired."

"Do you need anything? Like a drink of water?"

She shook her head.

She lay there in silence, just looking up at him. He waited, his lips smiling emptily, thinking how small she looked, alone in the big double bed.

"You haven't had your supper yet," she said at last.

"Aunt Loretta's fixing it now. And she's bringing you yours upstairs."

She nodded.

He shuffled his feet.

"I guess I'll go downstairs now," he told her.

She nodded again.

He tiptoed across the linoleum.

"You might as well turn off the light now," she said, "and save the electricity."

He yanked at the thin, metal chain that hung from the ceiling light fixture. The room switched into darkness.

"Good night, now, Gran," he said.

In the kitchen, the table was already set. Aunt Loretta was dishing out warmed-over stew and potatoes, while Mary Agnes dangled Mr. Kinsella's present in front of his nose.

Timothy washed his hands at the sink and sat down in his chair. He stared at the pattern in the oilcloth that covered the table.

"Just look at Mr. Kinsella!" Mary Agnes called to him.

He looked. But it no longer seemed to matter very much that Mr. Kinsella was going into fits of ecstasy over his catnip mouse.

FOUR

A Sunday with the Brennans and the Byrnes

G ran was the first one down in the morning.
Aunt Loretta was sleeping late after her Saturday
night date and Mary Agnes, who shared the bedroom next to
Gran's with her mother, had to dress for church in the darkness, with the shades pulled down, stepping over her mother's
discarded clothes, so as not to disturb her. She hadn't heard
Gran stir.

Timothy slept in the attic. When he heard the stairs creak,
he thought it was probably Aunt Loretta going down to get
the Sunday paper. Aunt Loretta always liked to be the first to
get at the comics.

When the two of them straggled down to the kitchen, all
washed and ready to go to church, there she was, fully dressed,
sitting by the window with a mug of tea in her two hands.
Mr. Kinsella was settled on a chair beside her.

"Gran!" Mary Agnes cried. "What are you doing here?"

"Having a cup of tea, as you'd see for yourself if your eyes
weren't still stuck together."

Timothy began, "But the doctor said—"

"Dr. Rosenberg said I was to take it easy," she snapped back. "And that's just what I'm doing." She took a long sip of her tea and leaned back smacking her lips with satisfaction. "I like it hot and black, and thick enough—"

"And thick enough for the spoon to stand straight up in it," Timothy intoned, finishing the sentence for her. He had heard her say it often enough.

"Well," Gran remarked with a twitch of her mouth, "I see you've learned it by now." She turned to Mary Agnes. "Is your mother ready for church?"

"She's still sleeping. I guess she'll go to the late morning Mass."

Gran looked disapproving.

"Are you going to church, Gran?" Mary Agnes went on quickly. "You can't go if you're having your tea now."

"Are you trying to tell me when I can go to church and when I can't?"

"But you're not supposed to let so much as a sip of water pass through your lips from midnight," Mary Agnes reminded her righteously.

"Well, for your information, I'm staying right here. And when I finish this cup, I'm going right ahead and make myself another."

"Do you want me to tell Father Halloran to come over and see you later?"

"I'm not that bad!" her grandmother flared. "When I'm ready to give up the ghost, I'll let Father Halloran know in plenty of time. Don't start worrying about the state of my soul, Mary Agnes. I'll take care of it during the week, as soon as I feel like walking over to church by myself."

Mary Agnes wriggled with embarrassment. She glanced at her cousin from under the brim of her hat.

"Are you ready, Timothy?" she asked.

"Let me look at the both of yous," Gran commanded. They stood fidgeting in front of her.

She remarked to Mary Agnes, "Your stockings are wrinkled."

"Oh, ish-kabibble!" Mary Agnes said. "They always are." But she turned her back on Timothy and pulled them up.

"I guess you'll do in a storm, the both of yous," their grandmother admitted. "Have you got your collection money?"

They nodded.

"And your prayer books and rosaries?"

They nodded again.

They were nearly through the door when she called out sharply, "Mary Agnes!"

"Yes, Gran?"

"Is that polish you have on your fingernails?"

"No, Gran," she answered. But she said it too quickly.

"I suppose you can lie to me if you want. But you better tell the truth to Father Halloran. Off with you, now."

When they came back from St. Bridget's they found Mrs. Sevchick in the living room with their grandmother. The jar of soup she had brought was on the table in front of them.

"I see doctor driving away in his car yesterday," she explained to them in her heavy Slovak accent. "I was take Fritzie for walk. So I figure I come right over this morning and see how my Mrs. Brennan feeling. I knew it was my Mrs. Brennan who the doctor come see." She beamed and patted Gran's hand. "But my Mrs. Brennan okay. She look okay to me, hey?"

Aunt Loretta, already dressed for church, was in the kitchen putting the meat and potatoes in the oven.

"You can get your own breakfast," she told them. "But don't

lay a finger on the dinner. I'll take care of it myself when I get back."

Mary Agnes got their breakfast—cocoa and peanut-butter-and-jelly sandwiches—while Timothy went down to the cellar and brought up a load of coal for the stove. Then they ate at the kitchen table, squabbling over who was to have what part of the Sunday paper.

It was a cold, grimy day outside and it had begun to drizzle while they were still at church. From the living room came the drone of Mrs. Sevchick's voice, with Gran putting in a word now and then.

How Timothy hated these Sundays in Duffy's Rocks! They were always the same: the Sacred Heart of Jesus, meat and potatoes with brown gravy, Maggie and Jiggs going through the same old routines in the funny papers.

On nice days it wasn't so bad. He could always go over to McClure's Point and find some of the other boys from St. Bridget's to fool around with, chucking rocks down the steep slope, trying to hit the barges in the river, and watching the rocks bounce instead on the roof of the ice house; and things like that, although there was no special boy he ever bothered to look for. But today, with the cold drizzle turning into rain and all, it was hopeless. Then, at night, just before they all settled down to listen to the radio (on Sundays it was always the Fire Chief on the "Texaco Hour"), there would be that last spurt of homework which he had to get ready for Monday. And after that there was the whole week ahead of him, until another Saturday crawled into sight.

"I go home now, Mrs. Brennan," Mrs. Sevchick was saying to Gran. "I got to feed my Fritzie. Is very bad dog, that Fritzie, I tell you. Yesterday is run away. I go all around block two times in the dark before I find that devil."

So that was where Mrs. Sevchick had been, Timothy thought, when he went over to find her yesterday.

"Good-bye, Mrs. Brennan. You take everything easy, you hear? And I come see you tomorrow." Then, as she was going out the door, she called out, "Look, Mrs. Brennan, you got company!"

Timothy and Mary Agnes dropped the funny papers and went to the window.

An old blue Hudson Terraplane was parked in front of the house. It was Uncle Matt's car, with Aunt Anna, Gran's oldest, and her husband Matthew, and their two sons getting out of it.

And then the house was suddenly full of people and bustle. Aunt Anna came in first wearing her good hat and her old fur-trimmed coat. She was carrying a big agate-ware roasting pan. Regis and Leo, in their good, Sunday blue-serge suits, their hair combed into careful pompadours, barged in after her. Regis held a covered aluminum cooking pot and Leo had a big cake plate protected by a brown paper bag.

"Go easy with that cake, Leo," Aunt Anna screamed over her shoulder. "It's not a football. I don't want the icing to stick to the waxed paper."

Uncle Matt marched in last. His heavy tread was one which Timothy would have known anywhere. He was a big man, red-faced and grizzled. His dark Sunday suit and white shirt and electric-blue tie didn't seem to belong on his burly body.

Aunt Anna went straight into the kitchen and set the roasting pan on top of the range. Then she took the pot from Regis and the cake plate from Leo and put them on the table. After that she came back into the parlor and took off her coat and hat, while Uncle Matt and the boys stood around awkwardly. Timothy and his cousins grinned at each other.

"Loretta called last night and told us," Aunt Anna said to her mother, "so we figured we might as well come over and eat with you." She settled her tightly corseted body on the couch. "How're you feeling, Ma? You look kind of pale to me."

"I'm all right," Gran told her firmly. "I was just a little tired, that's all."

"Don't tell me you were just a little tired, Ma. I know you and your ways. You don't send for Dr. Rosenberg to come all the way over to Duffy's Rocks if you're just a little tired."

The boys went over and kissed their grandmother.

"Aren't you going to kiss Mary Agnes?" Aunt Anna said.

"Aw, Ma!" said Leo. "Do we have to?"

Uncle Matt and Aunt Anna laughed loudly, while Mary Agnes stood in the doorway as stiff as a broom and looked dignified.

"Whew!" Aunt Anna said. "Isn't this weather awful? I just finished saying to Matt, Ma, that every time we decide to take that car out for a little spin, it gets like this."

"Anyway," said Gran, "I see you still have the car."

"Sure," Uncle Matt said dourly. "But it's another thing to find the money to buy the gas to run it."

Aunt Anna, who had been pinching Mary Agnes' arm to see if she'd put on any more weight, turned back to Gran. "What did the doctor say, anyway?" she wanted to know. Then she said, "Don't tell me. I'll hear all about it from Loretta." She looked around. "Where is she? Don't tell me she's still sleeping. I'll go up and pull her right out of that bed the way I used to do."

"She went to church, Aunt Anna," Mary Agnes put in hurriedly. "She went by herself. Timothy and I went earlier."

"Don't tell me you went too, Ma? In this weather, and after what happened yesterday? Father Halloran could just as well have come over—"

"I wish everybody would stop worrying about me," Gran said in a brusque voice. "Nobody elected you Pope, Anna. I'll send for Father Halloran when the time comes. In the meantime, I have my own little prayer that I say."

Aunt Anna's eyes traveled over toward the wall, to the framed text in its border of shamrocks. "You and your Irish prayer, Ma!" she laughed.

"And I'd like to know what's wrong with my Irish prayer?" Gran sniffed. "It's carried me through all these years, it'll carry me through a few more. I remember the day when Bart brought that home to me. He was only a boy, but he went out and bought it with his own money."

Aunt Anna heaved herself off the couch. "Well," she said, "it's good to get my weight off my feet, but I'd better waltz myself into the kitchen and see what Loretta fixed."

Uncle Matt lowered his bulk carefully into a chair. Regis and Leo sat down unobtrusively. Timothy knew that he ought to say something to them, but he wasn't really sure what. They never had much to say to him. Regis was the older of the two, sixteen already, and not much interested in anything but athletics. He was already counting on going into the construction business, with the firm where Uncle Matt was a foreman. Of course, he'd have to finish high school first, and times would have to get better. Leo was younger than Timothy by a few months. He was freckled and fresh-faced, like his mother, and fat like her, and light on his feet.

"Well, and how's business these days, Matthew?" Gran asked.

Uncle Matt crossed his heavy legs. "I'll tell you how's business. There just isn't any to speak of." He leaned back. "And it's not only here. Things're bad all over. I guess Roosevelt's doing his best to end this depression, but he's not doing enough and he's not doing it fast enough. I tell you, when you see good able-bodied men with skills, and willing to work for next to nothing, sitting around on the benches in the park all day long, going to rot because they haven't got jobs, and they don't want to go home and hear the kids yelling for food and the wife nagging for him to go out and get work, the country's in a bad way." He shook his head, recrossed his legs, and sat staring at the wall. Timothy noticed that one of his shoes had a hole the size of a half dollar in the sole.

"We've had hard times before," Gran said. "I can remember—when was it?—"

"They weren't like this," he cut angrily. "And not one of them that went on for so long as this. I still go to my office, but all I do is sit there and read the paper. And when the men come around looking for a day's work, I'm the one who has to look them in the eye and tell them there's nothing. They're willing to sweep the place out for me, just to do something and have an excuse to be somewhere. I tell you, it's rough. I don't know how Anna manages on what I bring home to her every Friday. Oh yeah. I forgot something. Regis, go and get that basket. I left it in the car."

"Sure, Pop," Regis said promptly. "I'll bring it in."

Regis went out. When he came back he was lugging a bushel basket, half full of apples.

"I figured you could use some," Uncle Matt told Gran. "I got a few bushels the other day from one of my ex-customers. Ex only because he don't have anymore jobs for me these days. Take 'em into the kitchen, Regis. Your mother'll know where to put them."

Gran said, "Things can't go on forever like this, Matthew. We've been through times like this before. We always manage to pull out of them somehow."

Uncle Matt sighed and unbuttoned his vest.

"That's what they all say. Prosperity is just around the corner. But like whats-his-name was saying on the radio the other day, he'd like to know what corner it is so's he could go out and stake a claim on it." He let out a sour laugh.

Aunt Loretta came bursting into the house.

"Why, hello, there, Matthew me boyo," she cried. "I see from Ben Hur's chariot outside that you got here." She bent over to kiss him, rumpling his hair as she did so. He smoothed it down at once. She winked at Regis and Leo. They grinned back at her. "Where's Anna? In the kitchen, I bet. Anna! Hey, what are you doing in there?"

"Hay is for horses," Anna called back. "I'm getting the dinner ready. I figured we might as well eat early."

Gran started to get up from her chair.

"You stay right there, Ma," Loretta told her. "Keep the football team company on the bench."

She threw off her coat and scarf and ran out to join Aunt Anna. Mary Agnes got up and followed her. Timothy, sitting there, could hear Anna and Loretta chattering like a couple of girls while they got everything ready, with Mary Agnes' voice chipping in now and again. Then there was the rattle of plates and the sound of knives and forks being pulled out of the drawer. "You put these out on the table, Mary Agnes," Aunt Anna said.

The boys remained silent in their places. Gran tapped the

floor with her foot. Uncle Matt yawned, stood up, and peered through the curtains.

"This street's getting real run down," he remarked to Gran. "It looks like it's all Hunkies and Slovaks."

Gran pursed her lips and said nothing.

Uncle Matt started to say something else. Then he shrugged and turned to Timothy. "Is the paper handy?"

"It's in the kitchen. I'll get it for you."

Aunt Loretta and Aunt Anna were talking earnestly over the range. They lowered their voices when Timothy came in. He knew they were talking about Gran.

Uncle Matt put on his glasses and read the sports section, and Gran asked Regis and Leo about their school, while Timothy just sat there until it was time to eat.

The table held Aunt Anna's roast and her mashed potatoes and gravy, as well as Aunt Loretta's meat and potatoes. In addition, there was a big bowl of creamed carrots and peas. They had come in Aunt Anna's aluminum pot.

"There's more than enough," Aunt Anna said. "I'll take home what's left of mine, although it won't tide us over no more than a day or two, with the way those boys of mine put it away. Not that their father doesn't get his share."

"There's nothing like meat and potatoes to fill a man up," Uncle Matt said solemnly, loosening his collar.

"Well, don't go getting gravy on your tie again. It's the only decent one you got left for when you go to the meeting of the Hibernians," Aunt Anna told him.

Aunt Loretta pushed back her chair and went into the kitchen, saying, "I forgot something." When she returned she was holding a deep dish with a steaming heap of bright yellow vegetable in it.

"What's that?" Mary Agnes asked.

"Turnips."

"Turnips?" Mary Agnes echoed. "We never had them before."

"There was a special on them at the store," her mother explained as she passed them around.

Uncle Matt speared a hefty forkful. After he tasted them he said with a laugh, "Just pass me some more of those mashed potatoes, Anna."

Mary Agnes said, "They taste funny."

Leo snickered. "Only foreigners eat them," he remarked.

"They taste all right to me," Timothy said, but nobody was paying any attention.

"I was having dinner over to one of my girl friends the other night," Aunt Loretta announced conversationally. "She's on the Project with me. She's Italian descent. They had spaghetti. And you know what? She told me they eat spaghetti every single day!"

A ripple of superior laughter ran around the table.

"No!" Aunt Anna cried. She wiped her eyes with her napkin. "You're making it up, Loretta!"

"Sure they do, I could have told you that," Uncle Matt told her. "They can't live without it."

"Well," remarked Gran, "they're Italians, aren't they?" So far as she was concerned, that took care of the matter.

"Imagine!" Aunt Anna said.

Timothy said quietly, "Well, we eat potatoes every single day, don't we?"

This time they all heard him.

The remark was greeted with a shocked silence. Only Regis and Leo dared to laugh, and they only sniggered.

"Potatoes are different, my boy," Uncle Matt told him in a

stern voice, "very different." He turned to the rest of the table. "Hey, listen, who knows the answer to this one: What's worse than being Irish?" He waited for only a second before giving the answer himself. "Not being Irish! That's what!"

Timothy stared at the little stack of potatoes on the plate in front of him. He could not remember a meal without potatoes. The others went on talking, but he was no longer listening. He tried to imagine what their faces would look like if, like the writer he had read about somewhere, he asked for "herons' eggs whipped with wine in an amber foam."

Then he thought that if mother were alive and he lived with his father and her, the talk around the dinner table would be different. He was sure that it was, in other families. There would be intense discussions about books and—well, world affairs, and a million other things which Uncle Matt and Aunt Anna and Aunt Loretta and the others had never dreamed even existed. He wondered what it would be like if they had something for dinner that wasn't just meat and potatoes. He wasn't sure exactly what, but the sort of thing people ate in books. He tried to imagine Uncle Matt toying urbanely with a salad, but he couldn't. . . . It would always be like this, he decided hopelessly, on Sundays at Duffy's Rocks.

"Timothy! It's you I'm speaking to!"

Aunt Anna was calling to him from her place where she was gathering the empty dishes. "If you're finished, just pass me your plate so's I can clear the table for dessert."

Without a word he handed her the plate with the uneaten potatoes on it.

The dessert was Aunt Anna's big homemade layer cake, covered with swirls of marshmallow icing. "I don't know how it turned out," she said deprecatingly. "I made it in such a hurry."

It was delicious. But then, Aunt Anna's cakes always were.

"It's a good thing you brought it, Anna," Aunt Loretta said, her mouth full. "I was going to mix some chocolate pudding, but with the excitement around here, I just forgot to get it ready."

Uncle Matt finished his cake and pushed away his plate. "That one turned out all right, Anna," he said. "I guess I like the kind you make with the orange icing better, though."

Aunt Anna let out an exaggerated sigh of martyrdom. "There's no pleasing some men, is there, Loretta?" she said.

Uncle Matt leaned back in his chair and surveyed the room with its stained oatmeal-colored wallpaper, its golden oak dining set, and the metal chandelier with its frosted glass shades which hung directly over the table.

"Ever think of selling this house?" he asked, turning toward Gran. "The neighborhood was shot to hell even before the depression started, and it's stayed the same way ever since. I think I know somebody might give you a fair price for it. And my advice would be to take it while you can still get it."

"You listen to what Matt says, Ma," Aunt Anna put in. "He knows."

"And if I was to sell it, Matthew," Gran said shyly, "where would I go?"

"You could come and live with us," Aunt Anna said, "in Stowe Township."

"And what about Timothy?"

"There's plenty of room for Tim with us, Ma. He could share Leo's room."

"What about Loretta?" Gran asked.

"Mary Agnes and I'd managed all right," Aunt Loretta replied at once, glibly. "There's a girl friend of mine, you don't know her, she's divorced, got a big place all to herself. She's dying of loneliness. Only the other day she asked me to move in with her. I'd only have to pay my share of the expenses and no rent. She owns the house, you see, Ma. And her girl is dying to meet Mary Agnes. They're the same age."

Gran looked at Loretta for a moment in stunned silence.

"Loretta, now don't tell me you'd let your daughter live in the same house with a divorcee!" she said, after it had sunk in.

"We have to keep up with the times, Ma," Aunt Loretta replied lightly. "Everybody's divorced nowadays."

"Who's everybody?" Gran snapped.

"Well—" Aunt Loretta began.

Gran cut her short. "No one is divorced, Loretta, except Protestants," she said. "And we don't mix with them."

"Come on, Ma," Aunt Loretta said, raising her voice. "Just because we're Catholics doesn't mean we have to be prehistoric!"

Gran pressed her lips firmly together and said nothing.

Aunt Anna shot Aunt Loretta a significant look. Then she turned back to Gran. She said, putting the conversation safely back on its original course, "The money from the house, you could use it for lots of things, Ma. Like Timothy's college."

"When it's time for Timothy to go to college," Gran said, "I'll find a way."

"Well, what's the sense of staying in Duffy's Rocks," Uncle Matt went on, "when there's practically no Irish left on the street, all your old friends are moved away, and we can't get over here to see you as often as Anna'd like? And after what happened yesterday—"

Gran had been listening to him with an odd thin smile on her face. Now she held up her hand.

"I'm not leaving," she said in a sharp determined voice, "not until they carry me out. This is my house and I'm staying here." She turned to Anna and Loretta. "Your father and I bought this house in Duffy's Rocks when we were married; we worked hard to pay for it; we never owed anybody a penny on it. The two of yous and your brother Bartholomew was born in it. Duffy's Rocks is where they know who I am. It may be a little old-fashioned like you say, Matthew, but I'm a little old-fashioned too. As for the house, it's a good sound house still. There's plenty of wear and life left in it. And while I live, Duffy's Rocks and this house, please God, is where I'll live."

Aunt Anna and Aunt Loretta exchanged a glance. Aunt Loretta said, "Well, we can talk about it some other time," and got up from the table.

"Anyway," said Uncle Matt, "it won't hurt to think it over."

"I thought it over," she told him. "And I gave you my answer."

He stood up and went over to the radio and started fiddling with the dials.

Aunt Loretta began to clear the table. Mr. Kinsella appeared from nowhere and danced sedately around her feet, mewing for scraps.

There was a burst of classical music from the radio.

"What the devil's that?" Uncle Matt exclaimed.

"It must be the symphony concert broadcast," Timothy said.

"Symphony!" hooted Uncle Matt. "Where's my football game?"

He twiddled again and found it. Then he settled back in the nearest chair, opening the top button of his trousers. He belched gently.

Regis and Leo pulled their chairs over to the set and listened with him.

Gran moistened her thumb and forefinger with her tongue and sat picking the crumbs of bread off the tablecloth as she always did after meals.

"Why, Anna!" Loretta said with a giggle as she cleared the plates, "you're not eating another piece of that cake!"

"I'd like to see somebody try and stop me!"

Loretta, holding a dish in each hand, paused in the doorway on her way out to the kitchen and scratched her back against the doorpost. "Honestly, Anna. You ought to get yourself a decent girdle or something. You oughtn't to let yourself go like that."

"Oh, I'm all right," Anna replied, complacently patting her bulging sides. "Matt likes it."

"Well, all I can say," Loretta retorted, "is we widows have got to keep our girlish figures if we don't want to stay widows."

Through a mouthful of cake Anna said, "What's this I hear about a Mr. Constantino? Anything serious, Lor? He's an Italian, isn't he?"

"Serious? Who's serious? I'm free, white, and I'll never see twenty-one again. I'll go out with anyone who'll take me." She abruptly stopped wriggling against the doorpost. "That sure feels better," she observed. "I had an itch right there. You know. And that's when you really feel you need a husband, Anna: just when there's an itchy spot right between the shoulder blades that you can't get by yourself. And," she added, her tone suddenly turning bitter, "when you have a kid to support who keeps getting bigger every day. But I guess you wouldn't know. You've always had Matt. But there's times, Anna, let me tell you, when you feel you just can't go it alone anymore."

Gran stopped picking up bread crumbs and broke in at

once. "Mary Agnes," she said, "I want you to go out into the kitchen this blessed minute. Put on an apron and start the dishes. And you, Timothy, I'd think you'd be wanting to take Regis and Leo up to your room for a while."

Mary Agnes disappeared into the kitchen.

Regis and Leo obviously wanted to stay there listening to the game with their father, but they didn't say so. They moved away from the radio at once and stomped after Timothy up the worn stairs.

FIVE

"When Did You Last See Your Father?"

Timothy went ahead of his cousins through the open door of his room. It wasn't a room, really. It was only the attic. He switched on the overhead light, wondering as he did so if he ought to say something about the state it was in.

But Regis and Leo didn't seem to notice the lumpily made bed, or the schoolbooks scattered around, or his weekday shoes and socks left in the middle of the brown linoleum rug.

He tried to look at it through their eyes, contrasting it with the rooms they had in the stucco one-family bungalow out in Stowe Township. He could still remember when Uncle Matt and Aunt Anna bought that house and moved away from Duffy's Rocks. It was five years ago, in 1929, just before the stock market crash. Uncle Matt had been making good money in those boom days, and the Hudson Terraplane had been brand new then. Stowe Township was a fairly new community, out beyond the city limits.

Even now the house still looked new and shiny. Uncle Matt was always fixing it up in his spare time; and these days, as he said, he had plenty of that. The boys' rooms were big and airy with lots of closets. Their walls were covered with college pennants: Notre Dame and Pitt and Holy Cross and Villanova. They had tracked up glossy pictures of prize-fighters like Jack Sharkey and Jack Dempsey. There was also a collection of football players. Leo had a lot of baseball players as well. Half of the floor of Regis' room was taken up with his model electric trains. He had had those ever since he was a little kid too small to be allowed to fool around with them without Uncle Matt's supervision.

By comparison with their rooms, his attic wasn't much, Timothy guessed. It was really rather cramped, with the roof sloping down both sides so that you couldn't actually stand up straight in a lot of places. The walls were stained—not that it mattered much. They hadn't been any particular color to begin with. And what little furniture the room held was kind of rickety. It wasn't really the kind of place to do anything in, he decided, except sleep and get dressed. And it was always freezing cold in winter up there, while in summer it was so hot and stuffy you could hardly breathe.

Regis and Leo sat down on the edge of the bed.

There was an awkward silence.

"Well," Timothy said, "what do you want to do?"

Leo said, "I don't know. What do you think, Regis?"

Regis said he didn't know either.

"Have you got any cards? We could play cards," Leo said.

Timothy shook his head. He didn't have any. There weren't any in the house, for that matter.

"Or any games?" Leo suggested.

Timothy didn't have any games either. There was nothing for them to do but talk, and none of them seemed to have anything much to say.

"How's school?" Timothy asked at last.

"Okay, I guess," Regis said. "You know."

"Our football team beat St. Joseph of Arimathea last week," Leo announced.

They spent about half an hour discussing the differences between St. Bridget's and Our Lady of Lourdes, at Stowe Township. They agreed in the end that, as far as they could figure out, all parochial schools were pretty much the same.

After that the talk flagged again.

Then, Regis cautiously reached into his jacket pocket and produced some Wings. Timothy knew the brand. They were ten cents a pack, the cheapest cigarettes you could buy.

"Smoke?" Regis asked in a grown-up voice, holding the pack out to Timothy.

Timothy shook his head. Leo, when the Wings were offered to him, looked undecided.

"You go ahead and smoke if you want to, though," Timothy told Regis.

Regis deliberated for a moment. Then he shoved the pack back into his pocket.

"Maybe I better not," he said. "If Gran was to come up here and smell tobacco, we'd never hear the end of it."

"Do you smoke in front of Uncle Matt?" Timothy asked.

Leo let out a guffaw. "Nah. He wouldn't dare. Dad's strict."

Silence hung over them again.

"If it was a halfway decent day," Timothy said, "we could go over to McClure's Point and throw a ball around, or something."

"Yeah. We could do that," Regis said. "But it's still drizzling. So we can't."

"Anyway we can't," Leo reminded him. "We got our good suits on."

"If you had a radio up here we could listen to the game," Regis said, yawning.

Leo went and poked among Timothy's books. He found an old *Tom Swift* and started reading that. Regis picked up a book which Timothy had borrowed from the public library and leafed through it, looking at the pictures. It was *The Glorious Adventure* by Richard Halliburton. Its account of the winter's vagabond voyages to the faraway wonders of the world had filled Timothy's daydreams for a week. But Regis didn't seem much interested in it. After a few minutes, he tossed the book aside. "Don't you have anything about sports or aviation?"

"Gee, Regis, no. I'm sorry."

Regis stretched. Then he got up restlessly and walked around the room. He stopped in front of Timothy's old dresser and idly examined the photographs on it. There was one of Timothy's father, and a studio portrait of Timothy's mother taken before she was married. She looked young and pretty. She wore a hat trimmed with roses, and there was a bunch of roses tucked into the sash of her dress. Timothy came and stood behind his cousin, looking over Regis' shoulder.

Regis reached out and picked up the photograph of Timothy's father.

"The family movie star," he said. "The Arrow collar hero." He turned to Timothy. "By the way, where is Uncle Bart these days, anyway?"

"I'm not sure exactly," Timothy replied. "He's pretty busy you know. He's traveling around all the time on different jobs. He's an engineer."

"Yeah," Regis said. "I know."

Leo looked up from *Tom Swift*. "It's tough these days for engineers," he said.

Regis said, "I guess he must write to you pretty often from all those places he goes to."

Timothy's throat suddenly felt dry.

"Well," he managed to say, "he doesn't have too much time to write. When he does, he writes mostly to Gran."

Regis set the photograph down again.

He gave Timothy a searching, curious look. "Tell me something," he said. "When was the last time you saw him?"

Timothy felt the blood rising in his cheeks.

Both boys were staring at him now with unusual interest.

He turned his face away, toward the old photograph of his father. He studied the frank smiling face, wondering as he so often did, if his father had changed at all since the last time he had seen him.

When, exactly, was the last time he had seen his father?

But he did not have to stop and think when it was. He remembered it. He remembered every minute of the time, as clearly as if it had been a movie.

It had been nearly seven years ago. He was just a kid.

He remembered how he had come home from school that late spring day to find a strange man sitting in the parlor with Gran.

"Come over here, Timothy," Gran had said. Then, "This is your dad."

He hadn't seen him since he was a small baby, so he couldn't remember his face except from his pictures. But he had always told Gran what he would do the day his dad came home to Duffy's Rocks to find him. He would open his arms wide and rush over to his father and throw his arms around him, and then his dad would never leave Duffy's Rocks again.

But now that the man was here, filling their parlor, he suddenly became too shy even to shake hands with him.

He sat there, dangling his feet from the sofa, his mouth gaping, while his father talked to Gran. He had never seen anybody who looked so handsome and tall and who talked like his dad. None of the kids he knew had a father like that.

He had wanted to interrupt while his father was talking. He had wanted to demand, "Dad, tell me about—." He wasn't sure what: about everything at once!

But he had just remained there, not saying anything, grinning foolishly, while his father told Gran.

He recalled going out with his father after supper to the ice-cream parlor down the street, hoping as he went that all the kids on his block saw them. And his father bought a whole quart carton of ice cream! Aunt Loretta and Mary Agnes weren't living with Gran then, and the three of them couldn't eat it all. It wouldn't keep in this ice box, so what was left over melted and had to be emptied down the drain in the sink.

After that, his father came upstairs and sat beside his bed talking to him, telling him about the different places where he had been, like New York and Boston and Philadelphia and California. . . . Timothy couldn't remember them all, his father had lived everywhere. Until finally Gran marched upstairs and said, "Bart, it's time for the boy to get some sleep. He's excited enough as it is."

"I see the Ringling Brothers show is in town," his father said to Gran. "I'll see if I can get tickets tomorrow and take him."

He still remembered how the thought of going to the circus with his father had been so exciting that it hurt him in the chest. And after the circus, he had been sure of it, his father would take him away with him. They would go off together to New York and Philadelphia and California. . . .

And then his father bent over to kiss Timothy goodnight.

A terrible shyness suddenly came over Timothy again. He turned his burning face away, burying it in the pillow.

His father only laughed.

After that, his father and Gran went downstairs. Gran shut his door, but he got up again and opened it. He could hear them talking in low voices for a long time.

When he woke up in the morning his father was gone.

And that was the last time he had seen him. After that, his father had never come to take him to the circus and to all those other places.

Every time he asked Gran when his dad was coming back, she only answered, grim-faced, that he had to go away on business. His father had never been back to Duffy's Rocks since then.

All the time when he was still a kid, Timothy had wondered if it was his fault. Perhaps if he had let his father kiss him good night, he would never have gone away.

After that he had done his best to push it all out of his mind.

But as he stood there, it all came back to him so sharply that for a minute it was hard to breathe.

The eyes of Regis and Leo, curious and expectant, were still on him, waiting for his answer. They made him feel uneasy, but he did his best not to show it.

He looked up and faced his cousins.

"Gee, Regis," he said, shaking his head and trying to sound offhand, "I forget."

But the question stayed with him. It was almost audible in the room. Why hadn't his father come back? It couldn't have been, as he had thought when he was only a kid, that it was just because he had been too shy to know how to behave with him. There must be some other reason for the lack of letters, and for the long years of staying away from Duffy's Rocks.

Leo piped up, "My pop says that Uncle Bart is just—"

Timothy saw Regis shoot Leo a look. It was as sharp as a kick in the shins, and Leo shut up like a radio when the dial is turned.

Regis remarked abruptly, "Pop said something about getting an early start home. What time is it, anyway?"

"I don't know," Leo said.

Timothy said, "The good clock's in the kitchen. Aunt Loretta's is always on the blink."

Leo, glancing at his brother, said, "I guess we better go downstairs now."

Mary Agnes, the dishes all done, was in the parlor playing listlessly with Mr. Kinsella and the catnip mouse. Mr. Kinsella was getting a little bored with it.

The grown-ups were in the dining room. Uncle Matt had fallen asleep and was snoring gently in front of the radio, which was still on. Gran and Aunt Loretta and Aunt Anna were sitting around the cleared table, talking.

"Anyway," Gran was remarking, "there's one thing I can tell you. Sick or not sick, I kept them in all the time. I've never let my grandchildren see me without my false teeth."

"The word for them, Ma, is 'dentures,'" Aunt Loretta corrected her. "People don't call them false teeth anymore."

"Well, mine are still false teeth, and that's what I'll call them," Gran informed her firmly.

She caught sight of the boys and broke off.

"Are yous all finished upstairs?" she demanded. "Yeah, Gran," Leo told her. "We're finished."

Uncle Matt opened his eyes and grunted.

"Who's winning, Pop?" Regis wanted to know.

Uncle Matt blinked. "I lost track. I fell asleep, I guess."

"He always does," Aunt Anna declared.

Uncle Matt glanced out of the window. "The weather hasn't changed any. We might as well leave now if we want to get home in time for the 'Texaco Hour.'"

Aunt Anna bustled into the kitchen to collect her pans and the remains of the roast. "I'll leave the cake. Mary Agnes and Timothy can have what's left with their supper."

It was half an hour before the Brynes finally got into the Hudson Terraplane. "You take care of yourself, Mother Machree," Aunt Anna called from the window of the car. Uncle Matt started to say something to Gran. Then he seemed to think better of it, and they drove off.

Now, Timothy thought, there was nothing left of the Sunday but getting his homework done, and the Fire Chief, and then bed, and another week of Duffy's Rocks. But there was something else. There was the burning memory of the last time he had seen his father.

SIX

The Days of the
Kerry Dancing

By Tuesday the weather turned crisp. You no longer had to be like the Skinny Marink, running between the raindrops when you went out of doors. And Gran felt well enough to put on her coat and hat and go to church by herself.

After that the household went back to normal. The next day, when Timothy and Mary Agnes came home from school, the parlor curtains were down. And there was Gran in the cellar, brisk as a bee, setting them in their wooden stretchers.

"And it was about the time, too," she remarked. "If you let a week go by you can see the difference for yourself. If you let two weeks go by, even the neighbors start to notice."

"The doctor said you were supposed to take it easy," Mary Agnes admonished her. "You mustn't wear yourself out, Gran."

Gran's only reply was to snort, as she went right on tightening the stretcher clamps, "It's better to wear out than to rust."

On Saturday morning Timothy went downtown by himself. Mary Agnes was going shopping for new shoes with Aunt Loretta, so she didn't pester him to take her along.

It was a bright day, in spite of the wind. The winter sun

shone through the soot, making all the windows of downtown sparkle.

Timothy wandered around in the streets with no particular plan in mind. But today nothing which was on display in the shop windows caught his interest. He considered going to the Carnegie Institute. Then he decided that he wasn't in a mood for that either. He had enough money to go to a double feature, but he didn't even bother to study the stills outside the movie houses. Not even the thought of lunching in solitary elegance at Mario's Continentale enticed him very much. He was too restless even for that. Somehow, this time, Timothy didn't feel his usual exhilaration at being out, alone, in the great world.

And then, as he turned a corner, he saw something which made his heart give a sudden leap.

It was a lady in a fur coat and blue hat.

He stared at her, almost expecting her to walk toward him and ask him if he could use a ticket for the symphony concert, explaining that she had an extra one and it would be a pity for it to go to waste.

Then she passed quite close to him without speaking at all, and he realized that she was not, after all, Mrs. Lachlan, the lady who had given him her visiting card at the last moment saying, "Do come and see me! I'm in the telephone book!"

Even so, he stood there for a while, remembering her.

The wind whipped an old newspaper against his legs, and people were jostling to get past him. "Don't just stand there, sonny," a man said in a gruff voice.

He finally moved off. He walked along quickly, trying to shove out of his mind the crazy thoughts that kept beating at him.

Why shouldn't he go to see her, since she had asked him to? And then, when he came to the William Pitt Hotel, he walked inside and made his way to the bank of telephone booths in the lobby. He found a directory and flipped through it until he came to the L's.

There it was, with the irrefutable reality of print: "Lachlan, Wm. C, res.," and an address on a street in Shadyside.

He fished around in his pocket until he found a bit of paper and a pencil stub. Then he wrote down the address and the telephone number.

What was there to stop him from calling up Mrs. Lachlan and asking if he could come to see her?

It was, after all, as simple as that!

And then he knew that he couldn't do it. Supposing Mr. Lachlan was to answer? Or supposing Mrs. Lachlan didn't remember him?

What he did do, in the end, was to hop onto the streetcar that went to Shadyside.

Shadyside was an established suburb and one of Pittsburgh's oldest. You could see that at once. It was different from Squirrel Hill. For one thing, the houses there were bigger and more solid. They looked as though they had always been there, each set out at a considerable distance from its neighbors. Even the omnipresent soot didn't dare to come out as far as Shadyside—at least that was the impression Timothy got. Tall trees lined the streets, their branches meeting overhead like the arches of a cathedral. There were real squirrels dashing around them! And there were no Catholic churches in Shadyside.

He asked directions until he came to the street and number he had found in the telephone book. The house itself was rather dwarfed by the ones on either side of it, but it was still substantial, with heavy draperies and pots of Boston fern in all the first floor windows so that you couldn't make out at all, from the street, what was inside. The draperies made him feel even more shut out.

He stood there waiting for— He wasn't quite sure what it was that he was really waiting for. What had he actually hoped to find, coming all the way out here?

His thoughts churned around.

Perhaps Mrs. Lachlan would part the curtains and look out and realize who he was and make him come inside. . . . Or Mr. Lachlan might come to water the plants and catch a glimpse of him, "Who is that interesting-looking boy? He has such a sensitive expression!" "Where? Why, that must be the young man I gave a ticket to, for the symphony. He appreciated that music so much that. . . ." Or perhaps they would just happen to come home from a drive and see him there, and then. . . .

And then, in the end, they would adopt him and send him to boarding school, and after that to the college of their choice— Mr. Lachlan's old Alma Mater.

But none of the things which he had imagined occurred.

There was no sign of life whatever in the Lachlan residence.

He tried to imagine what it would be like inside, since the only houses like that which he had seen the interiors of had been in movies.

Then something did happen.

Some people got out of a Pierce Arrow and glanced at him before going into a house down the street. He was sure they had looked at him suspiciously. They were probably telephoning the Lachlans about him this minute. Or the police!

There was nothing left to do now but trudge back to the streetcar.

He had a funny sensation of emptiness in him, and it wasn't only because he had not eaten anything since breakfast. He thought of picking up a sandwich or something downtown, but at the bridge he changed his mind and boarded the car which would take him to Duffy's Rocks.

The hollow feeling stayed in him all during the long ride home.

More than ever Duffy's Rocks seemed as though it had been put together out of old sheets of tin and cardboard, and his grandmother's house looked even smaller and sootier than when he had left it. All his thoughts were with the house on the tree-cathedraled street in Shadyside.

Gran was alone. Mary Agnes and Aunt Loretta were still out shopping.

Gran's face lit up when Timothy came into the house.

"I didn't expect you back so early," she told him. Then, peering at his face, "Are you hungry?"

He shrugged.

She brewed a fresh pot of tea and got out the loaf of soda bread, cutting it into thick slices which she spread with butter and jam. She poured the milk into a pitcher, which made Timothy smile to himself, remembering how she never permitted a milk bottle to stand on the table. That was one of the things she said was "common." Then she spread a square of clean white linen over the oilcloth of the kitchen table and set everything out on it. When she finished doing that, she turned on the ceiling light.

Timothy blinked, not so much at the light as at the extravagance of having it on during the day.

"Isn't it too early for that, Gran?" he asked.

"Go on with you," she said cheerfully. "As though we couldn't have a bit of brightness in our lives! We're not that poor."

His eyes caught sight of something blue pinned to the front of her dress.

"Gran," he exclaimed. "You're wearing my pin!"

She pretended to bridle. "And why shouldn't I? I guess there's no law against an old lady trying to look nice for her grandson, is there?"

He sat down with her and ate the bread and jam, washing it down with gulps of strong Irish tea, while she watched him. Mr. Kinsella jumped onto her lap and sat there, purring.

The tea warmed him. The bread and jam filled him. He looked at her across the table. Her hair was soft around her face. The light from the bulb in the ceiling was reflected in her glasses, making her eyes look bright and young.

"Did you have enough?" she asked. "I could cut you some more off the loaf if you wanted it."

He shook his head. "That was just right," he said.

Gran started humming to herself under her breath.

"Why don't you sing for me, Gran?" he said suddenly. "The way you used to."

"Sing?" She laughed. "Ah, Timothy. I've no voice left."

"Ah, come on, Gran. Nobody'll hear but me. Anyway, it's like a party now, with just the two of us."

"And Mr. Kinsella!" she reminded him.

"And Mr. Kinsella!" he granted.

"Is there any special song you'd like me to sing for you, then?"

"You know which one," he told her.

"That one? Again?"

He nodded eagerly. "Why not, Gran? You haven't forgotten it, have you?"

"But Timothy," she protested, "It's not the only song your old Gran knows."

"Ah, Gran, sing it for me anyway," he pleaded. "I feel like hearing it now."

"We used to have it on a Victrola record," she recalled, passing her palm across her forehead. "Your grandad brought it home one payday."

"What happened to the record, Gran?"

"I don't know. I think it was your father must have broken it." She laughed. "He was a terrible one, your dad, for getting into mischief. He was the Devil's stocking, if ever a boy was." She sat there smiling at the thought.

"Gran?"

"What is it, Timothy?" she answered after a moment.

"Tell me," he said. "What's he like?"

"Who?"

"You know who."

"Ah, you're always asking that!"

"I know. But you never really tell me. No one ever tells me about him. What is he really like, my dad?"

"What can I tell you?" She stroked Mr. Kinsella's ears. "God forgive me for it, but your father was the one I loved the most out of all of them. I never made any secret of that, although God in heaven knows there was times when maybe I shouldn't have shown it so much. Oh, it wasn't only because he was the only boy and knew the way to twist me around his little finger from the day he was born, it wasn't that at all. It's just that he always had a way with him, like. You know, when your father walked into a room it was like a light turned on in it."

As Timothy listened, the room was filled with his father.

"And he was always head and shoulders high above the other boys in the neighborhood," she told him, her eyes half closed while she spoke. "He was, like, different clay; and they all knew it. I made up my mind from the beginning that he wasn't going to waste his life and his spirit, like them and like his own dad before him, in the open hearth. He was built for better than that. So I scrimped on everything, and I pared the potatoes fine, and I saved what I could. I fought with your granddad, too, over it, I'll have you know. But I sent Bart away to college and made an educated gentleman of him, the way he had it in him to be. Oh, and didn't he act like he was to the manner born, always turning everything into laughter and fun!"

"Am I like him, Gran?" Timothy asked.

She looked at his solemn, eager face, and laughed.

"Like enough," she said.

"He was popular too, wasn't he, Gran?" he asked hungrily.

"Popular is it? Why," she went on, "the boys was all after him to join their clubs and socials. And all the girls was crazy about your father. Even after I packed his trunk and sent him away to college, there was girls I'd never laid eyes on before would stop me in the street. 'Oh, Mrs. Brennan,' they'd ask me, all simpers, 'and when is your son Bart coming home for his vacation?' And when he went into the Army, why, all the knitting for him and the letter writing that went on kept them all too busy to go out with the boys that was home!"

"And my mother?"

"It was your mother was the one that picked him in the end," she said. "She was a sweet girl and died young and it broke all our hearts when it happened."

He nodded gravely. Maybe now, he thought, the moment had come when he could ask her what was on his mind.

"Where is he now, exactly, Gran?" he coaxed.

Her eyes suddenly clouded, and he realized that it had been a mistake to ask that question now.

But then the expression on her face suddenly turned soft again.

"Ah, Timothy," she said, "I've talked enough for today. It's all ancient history now, like Battle of the Boyne. What's done is done. Nothing'll ever bring it back, and I haven't the heart in me today to rake up all those old ashes out of the past." She reached out and passed her hand over his hair. He knew that she was still full of her thoughts of his father.

Then she said, gently, "Well, do you want me to sing it for you or do you not?"

"Please, Gran," he said.

She began it in a thin quavering voice which was not always true. But as she went on, the old lilting Irish song they both knew so well seemed to lend strength to her singing:

> Oh, the days of the Kerry dancing,
> Oh, the ring of the piper's tune!
> Oh, for one of those hours of gladness
> Gone, alas! like our youth, too soon . . .

She stopped for breath.

"Go on, Gran," he whispered encouragingly.

She cleared her throat before she went on:

> . . . When the boys began to gather
> In the glen of a summer night,
> And the Kerry pipers turning,

Made us long with wild delight;
Oh, to think of it,
Oh, to dream of it,
Fills my heart with tears.

Oh, the days of the Kerry dancing,
Oh, the ring of the piper's tune!
Oh, for one of those hours of gladness,
Gone, alas! like our youth, too soon.

It was over.

The kitchen was filled with his own longing, a longing which was suddenly too great for him to hold back anymore.

"Gran!" he cried out. "Why doesn't he come back? Why, Gran?"

His grandmother did not answer him. Instead, she merely sat there, tears silently rolling down her cheeks.

"Gran!" he cried in dismay. "I didn't mean—"

She pushed him away.

"Gran!"

"It's nothing, Timothy," she said, without lifting a hand to brush the tears away. She just let them well up, misting her glasses.

"Gran!" he cried again. He jumped up from his chair. "What did I do, Gran?"

She shook her head at him. "You didn't do anything," she said. She bit her lip. "I don't know why, but sometimes my heart gets so heavy, I—"

He stood there helplessly, not knowing what to do.

"I'll be all right," she said after a moment. She brushed Mr. Kinsella off her lap. "Just go upstairs and leave me alone. I need to make myself another cup of tea before the others get here."

When he left her she was still sitting at the table, her old woman's tears still falling, falling as she stared straight ahead of her at the crumbs left scattered on the white cloth and at the empty cup beside them.

SEVEN

Shadyside

Through the week that followed Timothy was obsessed by the memory of the house in Shadyside. The image of it rose between him and everything he saw.

On Friday afternoon he walked home alone from St. Bridget's. He was halfway down the street when he heard Mary Agnes call out to him, "Hey! Wait for me, Timothy!"

She detached herself from a group of chattering girls.

He let her join him.

"Is anything wrong?" she wanted to know.

"No. Why?"

You got such a scowl on your face! Gee, you look as though you hated the whole world."

"I don't hate the whole world," he said savagely. "I just hate Duffy's Rocks and everything about it."

She looked at him wide eyed, not understanding.

"How can you hate Duffy's Rocks? It's where we know!"

He was longing to tell her, or anyone, about the glorious world in the visions of which he had been lost ever since he had gone and stood in front of the Lachlans' house. It was a world where—well, it wasn't that he was so sure what it was like. He was surer of what it wasn't like. In any case he knew that it was where he really belonged. Duffy's Rock's was like a pebble in his shoe.

But it was hopeless to try to tell Mary Agnes. How could he ever make her understand how he felt?

"I wouldn't want to live anywhere else, ever," she was saying. "Gee, everybody here knows us."

Anyway, he decided, he did not want to get involved in a discussion with Mary Agnes right now. He had already made his plan.

The next morning, when it was time to leave the house, he dressed with extra care. He spent a long time in the bathroom. He didn't dare to stay in there too long because you could hear the plumbing throughout the whole house, but he worked with particular attention on his knuckles and fingernails. He also took several additional minutes in front of the mirror, trying to get his hair to rise up in front in a casual puff, like Regis' or Leo's. But it was no use. His sandy hair was so fine and thin, it just stuck up in spikes when he wet it. Then he was ready.

This time he didn't waste any time in wandering around downtown. He was only there long enough to transfer to the streetcar that went to Shadyside.

As he approached the house, his mouth suddenly went dry.

It had all seemed so easy in his plan. He had imagined it a thousand times during the week. It was like something in a book, with himself as the debonair caller.

But now, as he was once again confronted with those heavy draperies behind the double storm windows, he wasn't so sure that it was such a good idea, after all. He was ready to turn around and go back. He could always spend the day at a movie.

His feet, however, were taking him right up to the house itself.

He was in front of the door. There was nothing left to do but to ring the bell.

Nervously, he thrust out his finger and pressed it against the bell.

A few minutes passed. There was still time, he reflected wildly, to panic and bolt.

And then it was too late.

Mrs. Lachlan opened the door to him. She was smaller than he remembered her, and she looked different without her hat and fur coat. Her short gray hair was set in neat waves. She stood there in a light-colored wool dress with white collar and cuffs, a pearl brooch at her throat, and a string of pearl beads around her neck.

"Yes? What is it?" she asked in what he thought of as her "English" voice. "We already have all the magazine subscriptions we need."

His mouth felt even dryer than before. Why had he bothered to come at all? It had been a crazy idea in the first place. She didn't remember him.

He managed to say, "I'm not selling anything."

She waited.

"I'm Timothy Brennan, Mrs. Lachlan," he blurted out. "I met you that time at the symphony concert. You gave me your card afterwards." He reached into his pocket and produced it, as though it were evidence.

Mrs. Lachlan stared at him. Then her expression changed. Her eyes twinkled.

"Of course!" she said. "What a nice surprise! And how thoughtful of you, Timothy, to have remembered me!"

Then she took him by the hand and drew him into the house, closing the door behind them. "You wait right here, Timothy," she told him, "while I just run upstairs and put away what I was doing."

"I don't want to—," he began.

"Oh," she assured him airily, "it was only a bit of busy work I had been saving for a lonely day."

She disappeared up the wide oak staircase.

As he stood there waiting for her to return Timothy had the impression of dark woodwork, polished so that it glowed, and heavy, old-fashioned furniture. He supposed that it was what they called "antiques." Everything was subdued in color. The draperies were pale-blue velvet; the rug, the sofa cushions, and the upholstery on the armchairs were a blur of faded brown and old gold. In solid oak cases, behind thick glass doors, there were sets of books, bound in leather and stamped with gold lettering. A pile of *National Geographics* was arranged symmetrically on a table. A bowl of bittersweet stood on the mantlepiece. On the walls hung old-fashioned steel engravings, in massive frames, of highland scenes in Scotland. There were no holy pictures anywhere. Potted plants filled all the windows and were set out on every table. The smell of lemon oil hung over the furniture. And the house was warm.

It was also, Timothy realized, a smaller house than it appeared from the outside. And, although he wasn't quite sure what he had expected it to be like, he was somewhat astonished that it wasn't more beautiful. Still, he was awed by what he saw.

He wanted to walk around and examine everything, but he didn't dare to move from where he stood. He kept his hands carefully inside his pockets, to show that he wasn't touching anything, in case Mrs. Lachlan were to return without his being aware of it.

And then Mrs. Lachlan walked back into the room.

Timothy grinned awkwardly.

"Well, I can't tell you what a pleasant surprise this is for me," Mrs. Lachlan remarked. "I'm delighted to see you again. Mr. Lachlan had to go away on business, leaving me with the whole day on my hands. I had nothing interesting planned, and here you are, out of the blue, to cheer me up!"

Timothy waited while she fixed him with an intent, birdlike stare, holding her head slightly to one side.

"Won't you sit down, Timothy?" she said.

He felt as though he were walking on spilled sugar as he crossed the room and lowered himself into the nearest chair. It had a high wing back and was covered with heavy brocade. He ran his fingers over the material, relishing the richness of it.

Mrs. Lachlan perched on the edge of the sofa, her back very straight and her suede shoes pressed together. He felt her eyes still appraising him. He felt like squirming, but he managed not to. He kept his shoes planted on the rug so that the worn soles would not show. He was glad, at least, that he had taken care to polish them so well.

There was a silence in the room.

And then Mrs. lachlan was inquiring, "Do you still live in—where was it?—"

"Duffy's Rocks," he said.

"That's right," she said. "I remember now."

"I live with my grandmother," Timothy said.

"Your grandmother? I see," she said. She leaned forward. "Tell me about her, Timothy."

"Well," he said, tentatively. And then it all came pouring out while she listened, nodding sympathetically from time to time: about Gran, about Duffy's Rocks, about the house. He even told her about Aunt Loretta and Mary Agnes.

"And your parents?" she asked at last.

"My mother died when I was little," Timothy told her. "I never knew her really."

"And your father? Did he marry again?"

Timothy shook his head.

"And where is he now?" she persisted.

"The last we heard he was somewhere in the East, I don't remember now where. New York, I think it was." He said it guardedly, hoping that there wouldn't be any more questions about his father.

Fortunately, Mrs. Lachlan seemed satisfied and did not pursue the subject.

"And do you go to school there in Duffy's Rocks?" she asked.

"Yes," he informed her. "I go to parochial school—St. Bridget's."

"Oh, I see," she said. Her lips seemed to tighten sharply, as though in disapproval.

"Of course," he said, "what I'd really like is to go away to boarding school. That's the best way to be ready for college, isn't it?"

"I suppose it is," she said. She looked at her wristwatch. "It's already time for lunch!" she exclaimed. "You'll stay and have it with me, won't you?"

He was longing to remain, but he took care to say, "I don't want to put you to any trouble—"

"Certainly you'll stay!" she told him. "I'm so glad you decided to come and look me up, after all this time, and everything you've told me is so interesting! And it's no trouble, really.

Everything's ready. Mrs. Eubank, our housekeeper, isn't here today, but all I have to do is just go out and set another place and put Mr. Lachlan's chop on for you." She rose. Timothy, not knowing quite what to do, got up as well. He remained standing until she was out of the room. Mrs. Lachlan returned a few minutes later. She had put a flowered apron on over her dress.

"Well, everything is rather sketchy today, with Mrs. Eubank off, but I'm sure you won't mind, Timothy. We can go into the dining room right now."

The mahogany table was set with a pale-yellow cloth, and there was a bowl of flowers in the center of it. She waved him to a chair and then settled down opposite him. He noticed that she removed her apron before she did so.

There were lamb chops with mint jelly, and buttered peas, and little rolls with pats of butter on separate plates as well. And Timothy did not fail to take note of the fact that there were no potatoes.

He watched Mrs. Lachlan, and was careful to eat the way she did, and to use the special little fork at his place for the salad. Every time she urged him to take more he said, "No, thank you," although he would have been happy to accept another helping.

As she reached out to give the flowers in the centerpiece a tweak, setting them straighter in their silver bowl, Mrs. Lachlan remarked, "I'm sure you must be quite a reader, Timothy. Of good books, I mean." She gave him a glance of encouraging inquiry across the table.

"Oh, yes!" he said eagerly. "Miss Schroeder, she's the librarian in Duffy's Rocks, told me I take out more books than anybody else. She says she doesn't know how I find the time to read them all."

"I'm so glad to hear that," Mrs. Lachlan said. "Especially since I'm such a great bookworm myself. Mr. Lachlan says he can't find the time to read novels. He's forever telling me he prefers something 'more solid!' But I try to keep up with everything that comes out."

Timothy was about to ask her if she knew *The Glorious Adventure*, but she quickly went on.

"Well, not everything!" she demanded. "I don't much care for the degenerate moderns, always debunking everything. I suppose it's the fashion, but why go to all the trouble of turning over a stone just to point out what's underneath? Why must they dwell on the seamy side of life? I prefer to think that there is so much in our lives which is beautiful and noble, just crying out to be called to the world's attention. I must say that I do enjoy worthwhile authors like Warwick Deeping and John Galsworthy." She smiled at him. "I'm sure, Timothy, that you must have read *The Forsyte Saga*?"

"Oh, certainly," he said quickly. He could not bear to admit to her that he hadn't, although he did remember, vaguely, having heard of it.

"I'm so glad," she said. She flashed an intimate, understanding smile at him. "Who's your favorite character in it?"

He hesitated.

"Well, there are so many—"

"Personally, I think Irene is fascinating. She's the perfect heroine. Don't you agree?"

He nodded. "Oh, yes!"

"And Soames: there are times when I like him even better than Jolyon. Do you?"

He said boldly, "I like Soames very much."

"I often wonder what it is about Soames—" She was dishing out the dessert. It was stewed pears. "I'm sorry, Timothy, this is all we have. In the house we don't go in much for sweets. But I think there must be some cookies in the kitchen. You'll have some cookies, won't you? I know that all boys like cookies." She went out and brought back a cut-glass plate with several gingersnaps on it. Timothy hoped that now she would switch the subject from the uncertain ground of *The Forsyte Saga* and talk about on of the books he knew well, but she resumed where she had left off. "Well, and now you must tell me what exactly is your opinion of Soames!"

Timothy said recklessly, "He's very dashing, isn't he?" He felt confident that anybody with a name like that would have to be very dashing indeed.

Mrs. Lachlan put down her spoon.

"Surely not *dashing*? Soames?"

Timothy realized at once that he had said the wrong thing, but he did not dare to admit that he had been lying all along.

"I think that he was very dashing," he persisted stubbornly.

She looked at him oddly.

"Are you sure you've read *The Forsyte Saga*? By John Galsworthy?"

It was too late to turn back.

"Oh, yes," he said.

Mrs. Lachlan did not pursue the subject. She got up from the table. "Let's go into the living room now," she said. "I'll bring in the coffee."

Before he got up to go into the living room now, Timothy carefully folded up his napkin.

She brought in the coffee on a big Japanese-looking tray which had its own stand. There was a glass of milk for Timothy. He was disappointed. He would have liked to have coffee in a little gold-rimmed cup like hers. Mrs. Lachlan pressed the rest of the gingersnaps on him.

Then he felt that it was, perhaps, time for him to leave.

He got up.

"I guess I ought to be going home now," he said.

"Oh. Must you?"

"It's a long ride back to Duffy's Rocks on the streetcar," he told her. He moved out to the hall.

There was a pause. Then, "Would you like to come again sometime?" she asked.

"Oh, yes!" he cried.

"Then you must come soon and have lunch with us. I'm sure Mr. Lachlan would be so interested to meet you."

"I'd like to," he told her.

"When are you free? Of course I don't want to interfere with—with your school work and your duties at home."

"I could come next Saturday," he said. "I always go out by myself on Saturday."

"Very well." She smiled. "Mr. Lachlan and I will expect you then."

He turned uncertainly, not knowing how to depart.

"Wait a moment, Timothy!" Mrs. Lachlan said. She ran back into the living room where she unlocked a glass-fronted bookcase and removed one of the books. Then she locked the bookcase again and came back into the hall with a thick volume in her hand. She held it out to Timothy.

"I thought you might like to have this," she said.

Timothy shyly took it from her. It was bound in blue leather with gilt edges. Its title, *The Forsyte Saga*, was stamped on the cover in gold letters.

"Are you sure—" he stammered. "I mean—"

"I think you ought to have it," she insisted. "Wait!" She took it over to a table in the living room, and wrote something on the flyleaf and brought it back to him.

"May I read what it says?" he asked. "Now?"

She nodded.

His hands shook a little as he opened it.

"To Timothy Brennan," she had written, "in memory of a delightful Saturday, from his friend Grace R. Lachlan." And the date.

"It would please me very much," she said, "to think that it was yours now."

He mumbled an embarrassed, "Thank you very much." She smiled at him. He was sure that she was pleased that he had nice manners.

Then he said, clutching the precious book to his side, "Well. Good-bye, I guess."

"We hope to see you next Saturday, at twelve o'clock," Mrs. Lachlan told him. Then she held out her hand for him to shake. It felt dry and soft and cool.

When he left she stood in the window and waved at him. Then the curtains drew together again, and he went on his way to the streetcar shop.

He felt as though his feet were not touching the sidewalk. He was treading the clean sootless air of Shadyside. He was filled with a wild elation. This was better than just wandering around downtown. He had found his way into a world of books, of ease, of no potatoes; a world where there were no holy pictures on the walls, and where people took coffee in the living room after their meals.

He only felt ashamed of having lied about *The Forsyte Saga*.

He was resolved that he would start reading it that night, right after supper. He would learn everything about Irene and Jolyon and Soames. And next week he would dazzle the Lachlans with his knowledge.

There was the streetcar now. Pressing *The Forsyte Saga* to his side, he started to run toward it.

EIGHT

The Beauty and the Loving in the World

When he went into the house, Timothy could hear voices from the kitchen. He listened for a moment. Mrs. Sevchick was visiting Gran.

He hoped no one had heard him come in. He was not in a mood to talk to anyone just then, especially Gran.

He was about to start up the stairs quietly when he heard her call out, "Timothy? Is that you?"

"Yes," he called back.

"We have company."

Even though the company was only Mrs. Sevchick from next door, he knew that his grandmother expected him to go into the kitchen and greet her.

He went in. Gran and Mr. Kinsella and Mrs. Sevchick were sitting around the table.

"My," Mrs. Sevchick told him, "you look very nice. You look like you been out all day with nice young lady, hey?"

He blushed.

"Ah," his grandmother said, "give him time. He's not ready for girls yet. Did you have a nice day, Timothy?"

"Yes," he said.

"And what's that you have in your hand?"

It was *The Forsyte Saga*. He had meant to put it down some-where before going into the kitchen, but he had forgotten to.

"Oh," he said in confusion, "it's only a book." It wasn't a lie, at least.

He was terrified that Gran might ask to see it, but instead she only turned to her visitor. "The boy is never without one, Mrs. Sevchick," she said proudly.

"Where's Mary Agnes?" he asked quickly.

"She and Aunt Loretta came back from shopping. Now she's out somewhere with the girls. I think it was a picture show they were planning to go to."

"Aunt Loretta home?"

His grandmother pursed her lips. "She's upstairs, getting ready to go out tonight."

He shifted his feet.

"Would you like to have something?" she asked him. "Get yourself some Fig Newtons. And there's milk in the icebox."

"I'm not hungry," he told her. He took a deep breath. "I think I'll go upstairs now. I have some homework to do. It was nice to see you, Mrs. Sevchick."

"Sure, sure," Mrs. Sevchick said, beaming broadly.

Clutching his book, he sped out of the kitchen and up the stairs. The door of Aunt Loretta and Mary Agnes' room was open, showing a pile of Aunt Loretta's dresses heaped in a frothy mass on her bed. From the bathroom came the sound of rushing water. As he passed it Aunt Loretta stuck her head out.

"Who took my bubble bath sample?" she screamed.

"I never even laid eyes on it," Timothy protested.

"I don't mean you," she shot back, slamming the bathroom door shut.

It was a relief to get into his attic again and close out the rest of the world. He threw himself onto his bed and lay there. He thought about his visit to Mrs. Lachlan's. The quiet, ordered house in Shadyside was still around him like a shell, like a promise, like faraway music that clung to his ears.

It grew dark. He switched on the overhead light and opened *The Forsyte Saga* for the first time.

It was hard to believe that such a sumptuous book actually belonged to him now. He had never handled one like it, not even in the book section at Kaufmann's Department Store. It was printed on India paper, so thin that he had to wet his fingers to turn the leaves. He was not quite ready to start reading yet. He just wanted to gloat over it for a while, first. Even the leather of the binding had a special smell. It was not until he had his fill of the feel of the book itself that he turned to the first page.

"Timothy!"
It was Mary Agnes' voice from the second floor.
He pulled himself out of the chapter.
"What?" he yelled.
"Supper!"
"I'll be right down."
"Gran says to hurry up, everything'll get cold!"
He got up and tucked the book away out of sight under his good shirt in the middle drawer of his bureau. Later, he told himself, he would find a better hiding place for it. Then he went down the stairs, two at a time, to the bathroom. It had been devastated by Aunt Loretta's preparations for her date. He washed his hands and face and wiped them on a soggy

towel. He was sure that in the Lachlans' house everyone had a towel of his own.

Mary Agnes and Gran were in the dining room, waiting for him. Aunt Loretta had already left. "Hours ago!" Mary Agnes said. She wrinkled her nose. "That Patsy Constantino again!"

Timothy hardly heard her. He was preoccupied, wondering how he could get out of telling Gran where he had been. It was a good thing that Mary Agnes did most of the talking during the meal, describing in full detail the movie at the Bluebird. She and the other girls had sat through it twice.

There was stew for supper, with lots of potatoes in it.

"Why don't we ever have salad?" he asked.

"And caviar, too!" his grandmother said, putting on a hoity-toity voice. "And breast of pheasant under glass, and wild boar, and I don't know what all you'll be wanting next!"

"You don't have to be rich to have salad," he told her.

"In times like these, we ought to be grateful for what we can get," she replied pointedly. "There's some who don't have this much, let me tell you."

"Oh, don't start on starving Armenians now, Gran," he groaned.

She only gave him a quick look and said nothing.

In the morning, when it was time to shake down the kitchen range and put fresh coal on it, Timothy wrapped his book in a brown paper bag and hid it in the coal bin in the cellar.

He was positive that no one would ever come across it there.

That week, whenever he had to go down to the cellar for coal, he took it out of its hiding place and spent a little time running his fingers over the tooled blue leather of the binding and reading as many of the tissue-thin pages as he could. Then he would carefully put the volume back out of sight. He never spent too long down there. He did not want to arouse Gran's suspicions. At night, after supper, he sneaked it up to the attic and read it in bed.

On Wednesday night he hung around in the kitchen after supper. Mary Agnes had finished the dishes and was doing her history homework at the dining room table. Aunt Loretta was in the parlor, gossiping with one of her girl friends from the Project while she did her nails. He thought of going up to the attic to read, but it was too cold and lonely up there. The kitchen was the only really warm room in the house, and it was quiet. He decided to risk it and got *The Forsyte Saga* and opened it there. He was sure no one would notice. He had already taken pains to make a cover for it out of butcher paper. Gran was just sitting in her chair, tapping her foot on the linoleum and stroking Mr. Kinsella, who sat, blinking, in her lap.

"What's that you're reading?" Gran asked after a while. "It looks terrible thick."

Instinctively, he put his hands over the book, covering it.

"It's *The Forsyte Saga*, Gran," he told her.

He was already about a third through it, and was deep in the fortunes of the Forsytes. He had quickly discovered that Soames Forsyte was a lawyer, a deliberate, careful kind of man. Every time he thought of how he had bluffed so rashly to Mrs. Lachlan, declaring Soames to be "dashing," Timothy was filled with mortification. He agreed thoroughly with Mrs. Lachlan, however, about Irene, Soames' artistic wife. She was the perfect heroine.

"Are you reading it for school, Timothy?" his grandmother asked.

"No, Gran."

"You haven't had your nose out of it all evening, not even to come up for air," she remarked. "And what might it be about?"

"Gee, Gran. It's all about this English family," he began nervously. "It's a big family, and they're all rich, and—"

"Ah," she broke in, "I could tell you about the English. When I was a girl in Liverpool was when I learned all about them." She smiled and sat there, remembering.

Timothy was longing to get back to the Forsytes, but he was so relieved she hadn't asked him to look at the book that he prepared to listen politely, although he had heard it all before, a thousand times.

"When I see all the Irish here parading on St. Patrick's Day, going on about the shamrocks and the harps and the Irish Free State and all, and talking against the English, I have to laugh. If it wasn't for the English, where would they be? They'd still be living in the peat bogs and speaking the Gaelic, with nobody but themselves to know what they were talking about!"

He thought about the Lachlans, with their engravings of scenes from the Scottish Highlands, and the portrait over the mantelpiece which had a little brass plaque on the frame which said ROBERT BURNS. He said cautiously, "What about the Scotch?"

"The Scotch?" She hooted scornfully. "Oh, I know all about the Scotch! For all their airs they're no better than the Irish. They all come over here just as poor as the Irish, with nothing but their shawls on their backs. The only difference was they wasn't Catholics, and they knew how to get ahead. And what's more, they're as tight with their feelings as they are with their silver. They wouldn't give a crippled crab a crutch."

"But—" he began.

"But, but, but!" she flared up. "Ah, Timothy, you can but me all the buts you like, but that won't put any butter in the old churn."

He lowered his eyes to his book again.

But Gran and Mrs. Lachlan, the Irish and the Scotch, Shadyside and Duffy's Rocks, all marched back and forth between him and the words on the page.

Gran still sat there, tapping her foot and watching him, when he finally closed his book and went upstairs.

On Friday afternoon Timothy returned from St. Bridget's in a state of high elation. He had finally finished reading *The Forsyte Saga* the night before, staying up until long past midnight to do so, with one ear cocked to the attic stairs in case Gran was to come up them and find him at it.

He felt now that he had become part of that English upper middle-class family with its money, its houses, its possessions, and its own rebels against its stifling standards of property. As he walked home, the concluding words of the book reverberated in his mind like a line of poetry. They were about Soames Forsyte, growing old and struggling to understand his life: "He might wish and wish and never get it—the beauty and the loving in the world!"

It was what Timothy himself wanted to squeeze out of life. He resolved that he would never rest until he had found them: the beauty and the loving in the world.

He pelted into the house. It was silent. Mary Agnes wasn't home from school yet. He had seen her walking out of the schoolyard with Millie Garrell, so she had probably stopped over at Millie's to do her homework, or play with Millie's baby brother, or something. Gran, most likely, was at Mrs. Sevchick's. He dumped his school bag in the parlor and dashed into the kitchen. It did not take him long to shake down the range and shovel some fresh coal onto it. After that he took the coal bucket and went down to the cellar and refilled it.

Then he reached into his hiding place for *The Forsyte Saga*. He wanted to read the last part over again.

The book wasn't where he was sure he had left it.

He looked around desperately for it, but it wasn't anywhere in the cellar. There was no sign, either, of the brown paper bag in which he always wrapped it.

After a while, he stopped searching and went upstairs. He sat down on the sofa and tried to think about what might have happened to it.

Suddenly, Gran was standing over him, brandishing the book in her hand.

"Where did this come from?" she demanded.

Before he could answer, her arm swung out. She gave his cheek a crack with the back of her hand.

"Gran! Don't!"

"So that's where you go every Saturday when you get all dressed up!"

"I don't go there every Saturday!"

"Who is this woman?" she cried relentlessly. "Where did you meet her?"

"At the Syria Mosque. She had an extra ticket for the symphony and she gave it to me."

"A likely story!" Her mouth twisted in scorn and disbelief. "It's a sad pity when a boy goes off to strangers every week and then has to lie to his family about where he's been!"

"Gran, listen—"

She was beyond listening. Her eyes were blazing.

He stared at her. Her hair had escaped from its neat bun,

and her glasses were crooked. She suddenly hurled the book across the room.

"Gran!"

She flung her hands up over her contorted face.

"Don't you come near me now. Let me alone! I was the one who brought you up! And now you're grown the first thing you do is run to strangers."

"Gran!" he cried helplessly.

She drew herself up.

"You can go back to those narrowbacks if you want to," she told him bitterly. "Forget that I loved you and took care of you since you was too small to crawl. But don't expect anything out of them. They'll never take you in when you need them. All you'll ever get out of them is that!" She pointed a contemptuous finger toward the volume. It lay at the foot of the chair with one blue leather cover flipped open like a broken wing.

He started to speak, but the words would not come out of his mouth.

She went over and picked up the book. Then she headed for the kitchen.

"Gran! What are you going to do with it?"

"You stay here."

"No, Gran. Don't!"

She grimly shoved him aside.

He stood there, hearing her feet go out into the kitchen. The he heard one of the lids of the range clank open and shut again. When she returned, her hands were empty.

"You can tell them for me when you go there again that it's too late!" She flung the angry words at him recklessly. "You can tell them they're not buying the grandson of Margaret

Brennan with all their fancy books and inscriptions. Tell them that if you want! And tell yourself that there's only one way to the easy life and that's to work for it and get it yourself!"

He told himself that he would never forgive her for what she had done. It was not only the book which Mrs. Lachlan had given him that she had destroyed. It was all the beauty and the loving in the world.

Silently, he moved away and left her there.

NINE

A Truce

"Hey, what's going on in this house, anyway?"
Aunt Loretta got up and stood with her hands on her
hips surveying the breakfast table.

No one answered.

"Last night the place was a regular morgue, with Timothy
not coming down for supper and Herself looking like the day
of doom. And now the both of you behaving as though you
didn't know where the body was going to be buried! What's
gotten into the two of you?"

Mary Agnes was stirring a small heap of sugar into her
oat-meal. "Timothy's just practicing being black Irish," she piped
up.

Timothy glowered.

"You hold your peace, Mary Agnes," Gran said sternly. It's
no concern of yours."

"Oh, leave the child alone," Aunt Loretta told her. "No one
can even crack a joke around here this morning. Well, it's a
good thing I have to put in some overtime at the Project today, otherwise I'd stay over for the funeral. So long, Oolong!"

"Overtime with Mr. Patsy Constantino would be more like
it," remarked Gran sourly.

Aunt Loretta gulped down the rest of her coffee and banged out of the house.

The others finished their breakfast in glum silence, Timothy and his grandmother avoiding each other's eyes and Mary Agnes glancing up to stare at them wonderingly from time to time as she toyed with her cereal.

Then, Timothy pushed back his chair and went over to Mrs. Sevchick's to take care of her furnace.

When he returned to the house, he went straight upstairs to the attic.

Mary Agnes had already gone off somewhere when it was time for him to leave the house, and Gran was still sitting in the kitchen. He braced himself against her pleading with him not to go to the Lachlans. He thought that she might even try to stop him.

But she said nothing. She went on grimly drinking her tea and pointedly not looking at him. She let him go without a word.

The streetcar ride seemed endless to him that Saturday. Every traffic light on the way seemed bent on impeding him; and everyone who boarded the car had to get change, jamming up the entrance, so that there was a wait at every stop before the conductor could yank the signal cord for the driver to start up again. And then, after he reached downtown, he had to wait several extra minutes before a Shadyside car came along.

He was impatient to get there. He couldn't help wondering what there would be for lunch this time. But that, of course, wasn't the main thing that occupied his thoughts. He was determined that this time he would not just sit there like a lump from the sticks, saying "Oh, yes," and "Oh, no." He would dazzle them with his knowledge and understanding of *The*

Forsyte Saga. He reflected that perhaps they had not read any of Richard Halliburton's books. He would recommend *The Royal Road to Romance* and *The Glorious Adventure* to them, and they would be very grateful to him for that. "What a well-read young man you are, Timothy!" Mrs. Lachlan would say then, impressed.

The wind was with him and he walked fast.

There it was at last: the Lachlans' residence.

He rang the doorbell confidently.

This time it was Mr. Lachlan who opened the door. He was a spare, white-haired man with gold-rimmed spectacles, a neat moustache and pale peering eyes. He had on a pepper-and-salt suit with a plaid wool tie. Across his vest stretched a thin, gold watch chain.

"Oh," he said. "So it's my wife's young friend. You're early." He pulled out his watch and looked at it. "It's only a quarter to. We didn't expect you until twelve. Well, come in, won't you? I'm Mr. Lachlan." He held out his hand for Timothy to shake. It was a firm and bony hand, Timothy thought.

Mrs. Lachlan came running down the staircase while he was getting out of his coat.

"Was that the bell, Will?" she said. Then she saw Timothy. "Oh," she said. "Hello, there, Timothy!" Then she turned to Mr. Lachlan. "I thought it might be Rhoda," she said.

They moved into the room.

"Our friend Rhoda Cameron is coming to have lunch with us too," Mrs. Lachlan explained. "She's a delightful girl, very talented, and I know you'll like her."

Through the closed doors of the dining room Timothy could hear the rattle of someone moving about, setting the table. He assumed that Mrs. Eubank wasn't off today.

"Well," Mr. Lachlan said. He looked at his watch again. Then he leaned forward and asked, "Would you like to wash your hands before lunch?"

"No, thank you," Timothy replied quickly. "I washed them just before I left home." He didn't want Mr. Lachlan to think that he had to use the bathroom.

"Rhoda's never late. I don't know what's keeping her," said Mrs. Lachlan. She went over to the window and peered through the curtains.

Mr. Lachlan subsided into thoughtful silence.

Timothy felt that he really ought to say something. He sat there, his hands pressed between his knees, waiting for an opportunity to come out with some of the many things he had thought of on the way over.

Mr. Lachlan got up and stood beside his wife.

"I'm glad she has her thick coat on, with all this wind!" Mrs. Lachlan said. She ran to the open door.

The girl who came into the hall was, Timothy guessed, about his own age. She was pale, with fair hair and thin wrists and ankles. She had on a coat trimmed with fur and a hat to match.

"Let me take your things," Mrs. Lachlan said, hovering over her.

Rhoda kissed them both, calling them "Aunt Grace" and "Uncle William." Then she removed her coat and hat, revealing a velvet dress trimmed with lace. Timothy noticed too that she was wearing grown-up silk stockings. Mary Agnes would have died of jealousy.

Timothy came forward to be introduced. He couldn't help feeling a little shy with this strange girl who entered the house with such an air of familiarity.

"This is Timothy Brennan, the boy I told you about, Rhoda," Mrs. Lachlan said.

Rhoda held out her hand and said, "How do you do?" like a grown-up. But she didn't look directly at him. She kept her eyes lowered to the carpet.

"I'm glad to see you're wearing our necklace, Rhoda," Mr. Lachlan remarked with satisfaction.

"Why, yes, Uncle William. I always do!" she replied, touching the gold chain strung with pearls that hung down over the collar of her dress. "It's one of my most treasured possessions."

"I don't think Mrs. Eubank is quite ready yet," Mrs. Lachlan said, glancing at the dining room doors which were still closed. "We might as well all sit down until she is. How was school this week, Rhoda?"

"Miss Fletcher gave me an A for my composition," she announced.

"I should think so! What was it about, dear?"

Rhoda's mouth curved into a remote smile. "I called it 'Confetti,'" she said.

"I hope you brought it along to read to us," Mr. Lachlan said.

"Oh, I *couldn't*," she demurred. "Not in public!"

Timothy was about to say that he didn't mind, but just then the dining room doors rolled open and Mrs. Eubank appeared. She was a stout, middle-aged woman with a red face. She looked curiously at Timothy.

"Lunch is ready, Mrs. Lachlan," she announced.

They all got up. Timothy waited for Mrs. Lachlan to introduce him to Mrs. Eubank, but she didn't.

First they had clear soup in little cups.

"I love consommé!" Rhoda exclaimed.

Timothy was startled to learn that the word, which he already knew from the menus at the Continentale, was pronounced with three syllables.

After that Mrs. Eubank brought in patty shells filled with creamed chicken and mushrooms. There was also buttered broccoli, and rice which was arranged in a big ring on the platter.

"Oh, Mrs. Eubank, you've outdone yourself!" Rhoda cried.

Mrs. Eubank smiled. "I'm glad you like it, Miss Cameron," she said.

All through lunch the Lachlans asked Rhoda questions about her friends and her school, listening with eager interest while she chattered away. Every so often they turned to Timothy and asked his opinion about something, but he sat there tongue-tied.

There was salad this time, too, and then Mrs. Eubank served the dessert: a large glass bowl filled with slices of orange mixed with coconut. Timothy gathered that it was called "ambrosia," and that Rhoda turned to him and asked, "I suppose you live out of town, Timothy?"

"I live right across the river, in Duffy's Rocks," he told her.

"Duffy's Rocks!" she repeated, looking at him with open astonishment—as though he had said Timbuktu or Vladivostok. "I've heard about it," she said, "but I've never been there."

Timothy fell silent again.

When lunch was over they went back to the living room, and Mrs. Eubank brought in the coffee tray. There were glasses of milk for him and Rhoda.

Now, Timothy thought, the time had come for him to astound them with his conversation, but he still remained silent, not knowing how to start.

"Aren't you going to read your composition to us now, Rhoda?" Mrs. Lachlan suggested.

Rhoda protested that she was much too shy, but the Lachlans

persisted, and so at last she took a folded sheet of paper from her purse.

"'Confetti,'" she announced. She added apologetically, "You must remember that it's only an impression." Then she began to read aloud in a curious breathless voice. It was as though she were reciting it, really, rather than reading it.

Timothy listened for a while. It was about snow, and how beautiful it was. It seemed to consist of a series of delicate descriptions of fragile snowflakes falling. Then his mind began to wander. He stared straight ahead of him, looking at nothing, while her voice rose and fell and rose again.

Then Rhoda's voice died out. It sounded to him as though there were going to be more, but she had finished.

Mrs. Lachlan sighed.

"That was lovely, Rhoda. Lovely!"

"I guess you're a born writer," Mr. Lachlan put in.

Mrs. Lachlan looked thoughtful. "You ought to send that to the *Atlantic Monthly*. I'm sure they'd print it. It reminds me of Edna St. Vincent Millay."

"Oh, no! Not Edna St. Vincent Millay! It's not nearly as good, Aunt Grace."

Mrs. Lachlan considered. "Better, I think," she averred. She turned to Timothy. "You haven't told Rhoda what you think of it," she said.

Timothy hesitated. "It's all right, I guess," he said.

Rhoda fingered her necklace and smiled.

"If you were writing about snow, how would you describe it?" she asked.

He looked at her.

He said, "I would write about it in a different way. I would try to tell what the snow is like in Duffy's Rocks." His voice rose without realizing it. "It's not like confetti there, where I live. I think," he went on, "that I would write about how the smoke from the Works makes the snow turn black almost before it touches the ground. I would try to describe the unemployed men waiting on lines in the streets for jobs they aren't going to get anyway, and how they have to turn up their collars against the snow, and stamp their feet on the sidewalk to keep warm." He stared at her defiantly. "That's what I would write."

The smile remained on her face, but it was as though she had gone away and left it there.

Mrs. Lachlan's coffee cup rattled faintly in its saucer. "Why, Timothy!" she said.

Mr. Lachlan leaned forward, his hands resting on his knees. "Let me tell you something, young man," he said. "The reason those men don't have jobs is because most of them would rather go on relief or boondoggle on the WPA than do a day's work. Any man who is hard-working and self-respecting can always find a way to support himself and his family."

"My Uncle Matt," Timothy protested, "says that—"

"I don't see how any opinion held by your Uncle Matt," Mr. Lachlan said frostily, "would alter the facts as they stand."

Before Timothy could reply, Mrs. Lachlan broke in. "I don't think you should argue with my husband about things you don't really understand," she said.

Timothy's face flushed. There was a tumult, a whirlwind inside him, but he fell silent again.

"But Aunt Grace," Rhoda said, "Timothy was just giving his opinion, and I think it was terribly interesting."

Mrs. Lachlan permitted herself to smile. "I really think we ought to talk about something else," she said. "You haven't told us, Timothy, what you did all week since I saw you last."

But it was too late now. Timothy knew. He should have never come in the first place. He mumbled something about not having done much of anything to speak of and rose to his feet. He stood there awkwardly, not knowing how to say good-bye.

Rhoda extended her hand. He took it, returned it, and then went out to the hall. Mr. and Mrs. Lachlan followed.

"You must come and see us again, Timothy," Mrs. Lachlan said as he struggled into his coat. "Perhaps at Easter you'll have some free time."

Mr. Lachlan held out his hand, then seemed to change his mind and thrust it into his pocket.

Timothy stumbled blindly out the door and into the windy afternoon.

The streetcar stop seemed miles away.

He didn't get out at the usual stop. He went all the way to the end of the line. He couldn't go home straight after all that had happened. He felt the urge to go somewhere, to get as far away as he could from the grime of Duffy's Rocks which surrounded him like the walls of a prison.

He shoved his hands deep into his coat pockets and started to trudge uphill. He passed beyond the outer edges of Duffy's Rocks, past the colony of corrugated tin squatters' shacks with its population of unshaven and unemployed men. After a few more minutes of steady walking, he found himself on a high open place overlooking the river.

He had made his way to McClure's Point.

He glanced around. There was a group of boys playing a listless game of touch football. Except for them, the Point was deserted. The boys were all strangers to him.

"Hey, feller," one of them called out. "Want to join?"

He shook his head.

He went to the far end of the one stone wall and leaned against it, looking out. Below him he could see the river. A string of barges moved slowly along its dirty brown surface; then there were the belching stacks of the Works. Beyond them, in the distance, shone the high buildings of downtown Pittsburgh. Beyond them lay Shadyside. And beyond that, in turn, stretched the whole world: the world he didn't know.

There was a strong wind blowing up there on the Point. It made his eyes smart.

Somewhere, out in that world, he told himself, was his father.

He knew now that there was only one thing left for him to do. He would have to learn where Bartholomew Brennan was, and find him.

With the back of his hand Timothy wiped the tears from his stinging eyes.

Where, he wondered, was he going to begin?

Gran and Mr. Kinsella were waiting for him when he got home.

"Well, and how were they?" she asked.

He shrugged. "All right, I guess."

She shot him a keen glance, and said nothing.

He went over to her chair.

"I guess I ought to have told you where I was going when I went there the first time, Gran," he said.

"Yes," she said. "You should have."

There was a pause before she spoke again.

"I suppose you'll be going to see them again next Saturday?" she asked.

He frowned. For a moment he had a wild impulse to tell her everything.

"Ah," he said after a moment, looking away, "what's the use?"

There was a longer pause this time.

"Well," she said quietly, as though she were speaking to herself, "the Dear Lord knows we have to learn for ourselves. Some are wise and some are otherwise."

He had heard her say it a million times. It always made him grit his teeth. But now, he didn't know why, he suddenly reached out and touched her cheek with his fingers. "Ah, Gran," he said. "You and your sayings!"

She covered his hand with hers, patting it.

Then she said, her voice stern again, "Don't leave your coat lying in the parlor, Timothy. Go hang it up in the closet, where it belongs."

He went out into the hall and hung up his coat. He wondered as he did so how long it would stay there like a threadbare flag of truce.

TEN

The Letters

From that day on, the idea of finding his father became an obsession with Timothy. It was like having a blister on his heel. He could think of nothing else.

Several times he attempted to interrogate Gran about him. (For Gran too, seemed to be aware of the truce between them. After that day she never opened her lips to mention the Lachlans to him. And on Sunday morning, when she went to early Mass with him and Mary Agnes, she wore the for-get-me-not pin on her coat where everyone could see it.) On each occasion when Timothy asked about his father he did his best to try to sound offhand, as though it were something he had just thought of, at the moment. When, exactly, was it that she had heard from him the last time? And where, ex-actly, had his father written that he was working, then?

But Gran was not falling into any trap. She was wary and evasive. It was as though she were playing Mr. Kinsella to his mouse.

"Ah, Timothy, what are you asking me all that stuff again for?" she replied each time.

"Oh, come on, Gran. Please try to remember. I want to know."

"But you know what your father is like as well as I do. When things settle down for him, after a bit, he'll be writing to let us know. I don't have to tell you that times is hard for a man like your dad."

"I know, Gran. But—"

"Wouldn't you have anything else to do now but to hang around me asking useless questions? If you've finished all your schoolwork for tomorrow, you could be reading one of your library books. When I was a girl in Liverpool we didn't have anything like Mr. Carnegie's free libraries, more's the pity, where you could go and get a story book and read it without having to pay for the privilege."

"But where are all his letters?" Timothy persisted. "You've kept them, haven't you?"

"I must have. I've never thrown anything away of your father's."

"Well, couldn't I just read through them, then?"

Her fingers drummed on the arm of her chair. "I don't think I could lay my hands on them right this instant."

"Why not, Gran?"

"Surely you know by now, Timothy, how everything is in this blessed house. You put a thing down somewhere, and the next minute it's moved somewheres else, and nobody can lay a hand on it. Like your Aunt Loretta's eyelash curler. And it's poor Mr. Kinsella who has to carry the blame for it all!"

"Couldn't you just *look*, Gran?"

She clapped her hands to her head.

"I have looked, I told you. And I couldn't for the life of me find the packet."

"Where was it?"

"In my room. Where else would it be?"

"But no one else ever goes into your room. Nobody could have touched them."

"Ah, that's what yous all say, the lot of yous, but nothing ever stays where I put it. Now how do you account for that?"

"I could go upstairs right now and look for you," he volunteered. "Maybe you didn't have your glasses on the last time."

She drew herself up in her chair.

"I'll be grateful to you," she said, bridling, "if you was to keep your paws off my private things. If there's going to be any searching parties turning my bedroom upside down, I'm the one who's going to be doing it."

He heaved a deep sigh. "I was only trying to be helpful to you, Gran," he told her.

She sniffed. He knew that sniff of hers. It always drove him into a helpless fury. "I may be getting too old to dance a jig," she informed him, her voice rising sharply, "but there's some things I can still manage to do for myself."

"All right, Gran. All right. I said that I was only trying to help you out."

"Listen to him! Well, there's ways and ways, and no-ways," she said. "And now, stop pestering me or else—"

"Or else what?"

"You'll have to try," she pronounced direly, "and see!"

Why, he wondered, was she suddenly being so difficult about the packet of letters? Was there something about his father that she knew and was trying to hide from him?

"Gran—," he began again.

"Sst! Off with you," she said. "I feel one of my headaches coming on. I don't want to talk about it anymore."

He left her and clumped up the stairs, wondering why she

couldn't be like the grandmothers in the movies, white haired and soft, always baking angel-food cakes and smiling tenderly when she spoke. And why, in all those years since she'd come here as a girl from Liverpool, hadn't she been able to shed that Irish brogue of hers?

After that, he noticed that the door to her bedroom was always kept carefully locked when she wasn't in it, with the key to it safely tucked away in the pocket of her housedress.

It occurred to him that Aunt Loretta might know something.

He waited for the time when the two of them might be alone in the house. And then, one evening after supper was cleared, Gran remembered that she had promised to trot over to Mrs. Sevchick's for a little visit, and Mary Agnes had to go around the corner to do her algebra with one of her girl friends. Aunt Loretta was in the parlor, doing her fingernails.

Timothy waited until she had finished brushing on the new varnish and had flopped back against the cushions of the sofa, pushing open the pages of an old *True Confessions* magazine with the side of her hand so as not to spoil the bright scarlet color which she had just applied. The stuff she had put on her nails made the room smell like a banana boat.

"Aunt Loretta?"

"M'm?"

"Could I ask you something for a minute?"

She made a face. "A person can never catch up with her cultural reading around this house!" she complained. "How the hell do you expect me to improve my mind? Well, all right. What is it?"

He cleared his throat. "By any chance do you happen to have any idea where my father might be, right now?"

She blew on her fingernails for a moment. Then she squinted up at him and frowned.

"What are you asking me for?"

"I don't know," he said. "I was just wondering about him, and I thought I'd ask you."

She waggled her fingers in the air. "This stuff never dries as fast as the ads say it does. What's gotten into you about your father all of a sudden?"

"It's not all of a sudden."

"That's what I figured. You think about him all the time lately, don't you?"

For a moment Timothy was too startled to say anything. Then, "How did you know?" he asked. "Did Gran say anything to you about it?"

She shrugged. "Herself doesn't have to say anything to me. I've got eyes and ears of my own. Anyway," she went on, "how should I have the foggiest idea where your father is? He never writes me. Herself is the one you should ask."

"I did."

"And?"

He jerked his shoulders. "She says she can't find his letters. I asked her several times, and every time she puts me off. I can't figure out how she does it."

Aunt Loretta laughed. "That's Herself for you, every time. If she has something that she wants to keep to herself, wild broncos wouldn't drag it out of her. And now she won't tell you where your father is. Well, all I can say is I guess she has her reasons."

"What reasons?"

"Who knows?"

"But if she won't tell me, how am I going to find out?"

Aunt Loretta sat, reflecting. "Look, Timothy," she said at last, "I'm not the one who can help you with this. All I can tell you is, whatever he is and wherever he is, she's the one who's to blame."

He stared at her.

"She's the one that spoiled him rotten," she went on. "I think you ought to know that much. He could always get around her to pull him out of every mess he ever got into. And it was one thing after another. He never could stick to anything. But no matter what he did, it was everything for him. He was the one she loved best, from the very beginning. Your Aunt Anna and I didn't count. We were just girls. But he was always her only begotten son, and no one was ever allowed to forget it."

He kept on staring at her. It was the first time he had ever heard her talk like that, with such bitterness, about Gran and his father.

"Just you listen to me, Sonny Boy," Aunt Loretta said. "If Herself doesn't want to tell you where he is now, you're not going to find out. But take it from me. She probably knows something that she's not telling. She was always that way about him: close-mouthed and stubborn. I could tell you—Oh, never mind what I could tell you. It's all past history, and what's the sense of raking it up? And what's more, don't you ever let Herself find out that I told you this much. If you ever do, I swear to you I'll get even!"

He gaped at her.

"Gee, Aunt Loretta—" he began.

She held up her hand. "For crying out loud!" she said. "You don't have to cross your heart and hope to die. You don't have to bother to promise me anything. Just keep your mouth shut.

And if you want some good advice, your old Aunt Loretta's the one who can give it to you."

"Like what?"

"Like this," she said. "Just consider yourself in the same class as Mary Agnes."

"I don't get it, Aunt Loretta," he said.

She let out a deep breath. "Sit down," she commanded. Then she said, "Look, Timothy. Its' simple. Don't ask me to draw you a diagram." She frowned for a moment, thinking. Then she went on, "From now on, just tell yourself that you don't have a father."

"But—" he gasped.

"Just shut up and listen to me," she said. "Mary Agnes' died. He was a nice guy, God rest his soul. I couldn't complain about anything he ever did. He never denied me a thing. He was steady and straight, a hard worker. And he knew how to have fun, too. You should have seen the two of us on the dance floor, too. You should have seen the two of us on the dance floor at the Old Hibernian Hall Saturday nights! But he's dead now. And yours," she went on in a harsh, blistering voice, "might just as well be lying six feet under for all you'll ever get out of him."

Timothy was mystified. He was also angry. His father wasn't dead. So what right did Aunt Loretta have to tell him that he might as well consider him so? He was thinking sullenly that now maybe he ought to talk to Aunt Anna. But what would Aunt Anna know that Aunt Loretta didn't?

Before he could say anything in answer, there was the scratch of his grandmother's key in the front door.

Aunt Loretta put her finger to her lips. Then she kissed it and flicked the kiss toward him.

"Don't take it too hard," she told him hurriedly. "I know it's tough on you, but that's the way it is. I thought lots of times how wrong it must be for you, growing up in a house like this with only women around you. A boy ought to have a man in the house to show him the ropes." She fell silent, listening to the front door. Then she added in a quick, conspiratorial whisper, "Anyway, if I happen to hear anything, I'll let you know." Her voice on its natural tone. "Well, I guess my claws are dry by now." She spread out her fingers and inspected them. "How do you like that for a color?" She laughed. "I guess I like any color, so long as it's red." She flopped back on the cushions. "Throw me my magazine, I have to finish my week's culture."

His grandmother shot them a curious, piercing look as she took off her hat and hung up her coat. But all she said was, "Where's Mary Agnes?"

"She went over to Millie Farrell's to do algebra," Timothy informed her.

"I think you'd better run over there, then, and tell her that it's time to come home. I don't want her out so late on a week night."

"Oh, Gran," Timothy groaned. "Nothing can happen to her. This is Duffy's Rocks."

"Really, Ma," Aunt Loretta protested. "There's no harm—"

"You do as I said, Timothy," his grandmother told him. "We're not shanty Irish, to be out in the streets all hours, like some I could mention. And don't forget to put on your coat. It's cold out tonight."

Without a word he got his coat and set out for the Farrells' house. On the way, he thought about what Aunt Loretta had said to him.

Did she hate his father that she talked about him that way? And how could he think of his father as dead?

No, he told himself as he ran up the Farrells' stoop and rang the bell, no matter what Aunt Loretta told him and no matter what Gran wouldn't tell him, he would still find his father somehow.

Mary Agnes opened the door to him. "I'm ready," she said. "You didn't have to bother to come for me. I'm perfectly able to walk home by myself. What'll Millie's mother think?"

"It was Gran sent me."

"Well," she replied huffily, "I can't help Gran's ideas."

They started to walk home slowly.

As they began turning the corner, Mary Agnes hesitated. Then she said, "Tim—"

"What do you want now?" He stared glumly straight ahead of him.

"Is—is something wrong?"

He stood there.

"What could be wrong?"

"I don't know. But, honestly, you're so funny these days."

"Ha, ha," he said in a gruff voice.

"I don't mean funny like that. You know what I mean. You can tell me, Tim. I promise I won't tell anyone."

He gave her a surly look.

"What's there to tell?"

"You can trust me, Tim," she cajoled. "I'm always on your side. You could tell me anything. They could tear my heart out with burning pincers before I'd ever betray you!"

He said with a faint sneer, "I see you've been listening to Sister Veronica's stories about those old martyrs again." Then, in the light of the corner street lamp, he caught a glimpse of her face: small and intent and earnest under her straggling fringe of dark gypsy hair, and he relented.

"It's my father," he said.

She let out a little gasp. "Has anything happened to Uncle Bart?"

"I don't know," he said. "Gran won't tell me anything."

"But you could always write to him and ask him!"

"She won't tell me where he is," Timothy said.

Mary Agnes considered. "Did you ask my mother?"

He nodded. "She doesn't know anything," he said glumly. "And," he added, "I need to see him."

"Is it something special? I mean, why do you need to see him just now?"

"I just have to," he insisted. "It's personal."

She waited.

"I have to talk to him," he explained. "I don't know how to explain it, Mary Agnes. I just have this funny feeling."

"I know what you mean," she said in a quiet voice. "You feel as though you can't know what you are yourself until you find out what he's like."

He looked at her in astonishment.

"Oh, I think about it all the time," she said slowly. "I mean, I watch you all the time, so I guess I know what bothers you. But if I were you I just wouldn't care about anything. If I were like you I know I could just do anything I really wanted." She nodded solemnly. "If I were you—" She broke off and blinked at him. "Timothy!" she exclaimed.

"Huh?"

Her eyes were very wide. "You're not planning to run away and find him, are you?"

He did not answer.

She reached out suddenly and put her hand on his coat sleeve.

"Timothy," she said breathlessly. "Can I help?"

He blinked back at her.

"I would, too," she declared earnestly. "Whatever you asked me, so long as it was something I could do."

"I don't know, Mary Agnes," he said at last. Then he brushed her hand aside and turned away. "It's hopeless. What can we do? Nothing." He stood there for a moment, looking down at the littered sidewalk. Then he said, "Oh, come on, Mary Agnes. Let's go home now. We might as well, before Gran comes out looking for us."

But it was Mary Agnes who had seized his thoughts out of the air and put words to them.

He found the letters the following week.

It was all a fluke. It wouldn't have happened, probably, if Monsignor Gavigan hadn't paid a state visit to the school. Sister Scholastica dismissed Timothy's class early, and he didn't feel like hanging around the playground. So he just went home.

He was nearly there when Mrs. Sevchick came barreling toward him. She was bundled in an old sweater, with men's shoes on her feet, an old white kerchief around her head, and a stick in her hand. "Fritzie!" she was calling at the top of her voice. "You devil! I kill you when I catch you!" She clutched at Timothy's sleeve. "You seen Fritzie?"

Timothy shook his head.

"He run away again," she panted. "Always he run away. I feed him good, give him good home. Why he no stay? This time I beat him good so he don't forget!" He watched her

chug down the street brandishing her stick. Then she disappeared around the corner.

The house was empty, except for Mr. Kinsella.

Gran had gone out somewhere—to church, he supposed.
She must have changed her dress first, because the door of
her room was open a crack. She had forgotten to lock it this
time.

He pushed the door open and went in. He began to rum-
mage through her drawers, looking guiltily over his shoulder
every minute, half expecting to hear her stern voice calling
out, "And what are you doing among my personal things,
Timothy Francis Brennan? That's what I'd like to know!" But
no one disturbed him, except Mr. Kinsella, who was feeling
lonely and kept brushing back and forth against his legs.

The letters weren't in any of the drawers of his
grandmother's dresser.

Then he remembered the old valise which she kept on the
floor of her closet, the one she had brought with her on the
long-ago voyage when she came over from the old country.

He got it, laid it on the bed, undid the worn straps, and
opened it up.

It reeked of camphor flakes. There was her wedding dress,
pinned in yellow tissue paper. Then an oversized, cardboard-
backed photograph of his grandfather, with a big moustache,
wearing a derby hat tilted over one eye and looking chal-
lengingly at the camera. There was one of Gran, too, taken
when she must have been just married. He didn't have time
to stop and examine it now, but he couldn't help noticing
with a pang how pert and pretty she had been, in her long
skirts and big feathered hat, and the feathered scarf around
her neck. He could almost hear her saying, as he glanced at it,

"Well, Timothy, you might as well be out of the world as out of the fashion!" There was a pair of baby shoes which he knew had been his. And a baby's white christening dress, thin and brittle, with a little card pinned to it which said "Bartholomew Brennan," and a date he couldn't make out. And then he found a packet of envelopes under an old plush muff. They were tied together with a bit of Christmas ribbon. He knew at once that they were his father's letters.

He was sure that what he was doing was a sin, but he brushed aside the rushing thoughts of Purgatory and what he would say to Father Halloran at confession.

He riffled through them hurriedly. He remembered most of them, postmarked from various cities. The most recent ones were dated from the year before last. And then a small blue envelope detached itself from the others and fluttered to the floor. He stooped and picked it up. It was addressed to his grandmother in an unfamiliar, pointed handwriting.

He turned it over. The sender's name was neatly written on the back flap. "Mrs. B. Brennan," it said. Below that there was a street and number in Brooklyn, New York.

His hands had begun to shake.

He slipped the letter into his pocket, managed to put the others back, and placed his grandmother's things over them so that it would not be apparent that he had been into the valise. Then he set the valise back into the closet.

His heart pounded as he ran up the staircase to the attic. He took care to close the door tightly. Then his trembling fingers tore the letter out of the envelope.

ELEVEN

That Woman

H is grandmother had a habit of waking up in the middle of the night or in the early hours of the morning and padding like a specter through the house in her nightgown. She would check the front door and the back door, letting Mr. Kinsella in, and all the windows. After that, she would make sure that all the faucets in the kitchen and the bathroom were closed tight, so that no water would be wasted. She would open the door of the room where Aunt Loretta and Mary Agnes slept and stick her head inside for an instant. When she had satisfied herself that everything was as it should be, she would creak up the stairs to Timothy's room.

There she would stand for a few moments over his bed, stooping to smooth out his pillow and to tuck the blanket in more securely over his shoulders. Then she would glide over to the window, which he always left open, and close it firmly against the night air. After that she would give the room a final survey before padding downstairs again to her own room.

Sometimes, Timothy would wake up and find her there.

"Gran!" he would call out to her from under the blankets. "Leave the window open. I can't breathe when it's shut."

But she would go ahead and shut it anyway.

When he wasn't too full of sleep, he would slip out of bed after she had gone and open the window again. The times when he didn't, he always had his nose stuffed up when he woke in the morning.

"You went and closed my window last night, Gran!" he would accuse her at breakfast.

She would nod grimly.

"I did indeed."

"Well, that's why I have a cold this morning," he would tell her.

And invariably she would reply, with the look of superior knowledge which invariably made him want to open his mouth and let out a wild yell, "You have a cold this morning because you opened that window before you went to bed. It was like an ice-house up there."

Nothing he said would ever convince his grandmother that closing his window for him wasn't the right thing to do for his good.

It must have been shortly after midnight when he heard her rustling across the linoleum. He kept his eyes screwed shut as she hovered over him so as not to let her suspect that he was still awake. He had not been able to sleep all that night. He had been lying there in the dark, listening to the shade rattle against the window sash. His thoughts had kept him in a state of turbulent wakefulness.

For one thing, there was the sin of having gone into her room and stealing the letter. He knew it wasn't just something which Father Halloran would let him get away with for ten Hail Marys. Even if he went to confession to the young priest, Father Brophy, who was known to be more lenient with boys, he'd still be in bad trouble for it. But mostly he was angry. He was angry with his grandmother for never having shown that letter to him. Or, at the very least, she could have told him about it.

The letter filled his mind ever since he had first opened it with shaking hands that afternoon and read it. He had read it over so often that by now he knew it by heart.

Dear Mrs. Brennan,

In answer to your letter asking me how your son is, I suppose it is my duty to write and tell you that Bart and I have not been living together for over a year now. This may come to you as a surprise that he has not yet gotten in touch with you to tell you this. Perhaps I also ought to inform you that he has also left his last job, with the Briggs Company.

Sincerely yours,
Mrs. Bartholomew (Marjorie) Brennan

He had hidden the letter between the leaves of a book.

All through supper he had kept his eyes balefully on his grandmother, wondering if he ought to confront her with what he knew, and yet not daring to say anything about it in front of the others. Once, when Gran and Aunt Loretta weren't looking, Mary Agnes had kicked him under the table and then grinned conspiratorially at him over what was left of her mashed potatoes. He ignored her. Later, Gran turned to him and asked if anything was wrong, and he only said, "No."

Aunt Loretta made a remark to the effect that taking meals at home these days was like eating at the morgue. But he just sat there, silently, pushing his food around his plate, not knowing what to say and thinking about how he could bring up the subject to Gran after supper. But after supper Aunt Loretta hung around in the dining room, letting down the hems of some of her old dresses, so he couldn't talk to Gran alone after all. He wondered if Aunt Loretta had any idea that his father was married to a woman in Brooklyn named Marjorie. If she did, it certainly didn't show on her face as she frowned over her stitching.

Now, as Gran bent over him to smooth out his pillow, he could feel the warmth of her body. He was aware of the faint warm smell she had when she had just gotten out of her bed. Her braid brushed his cheek. He clenched his fists under the blankets. He hated her. How long was it, he wondered, that she had known that his father had remarried, and she had never told him? He could never forgive her for that. He made up his mind to go on pretending to be asleep and not to give her the satisfaction of knowing that he was aware that she was there.

He heard her steal toward the window.

And then, in spite of his resolve not to let her know he was awake, he called out in a harsh voice, "Gran!"

She was beside him at once.

"What is it, Tim? Were you having a bad dream?"

"No," he said.

"Would you like me to come and sit on your bed and keep you warm?"

That was what she had always done when he was little and woke up in the middle of the night from the dream that soldiers were coming to take him away.

"No."

"What is it, then?"

He hesitated. Then he burst out, "Gran, I want to talk to you."

Her eyes were turned toward him. "What is it, Tim?" she

asked in a worried voice. "Do you have a fever?" She reached out her hand to press it against his forehead, but he shoved it aside.

He sat up in bed and stared at her through the darkness which separated them.

"The letter," he told her. "I found it."

"What letter?" she asked sharply.

His eyes burned accusingly at her. "You know what letter!"

"What are you talking about at this hour of the night?"

"The letter from my father's wife—from Marjorie."

She pressed her lips violently together. She said, "I don't want to hear that woman's name spoken in this house."

"You will now. Why didn't you tell me that my father got married again?"

"Married!" she cried. "You call that married! She can call herself Mrs. Brennan all she likes, but she hasn't the right. She's nothing but a—" Her thin lips curled with scorn. "A divorced woman!"

"All the same," he shouted back, "you should have told me. She married my father and I have a right to know."

"That's no way to talk to me, Timothy Brennan. After all, I am your grandmother." She was breathing hard. "Where did you put that letter? I want you to give it back to me."

"I threw it away," he answered.

"Don't lie to me! Where is it?"

"You should have told me," he repeated.

"Told you? Told you what? Did you stop to think what it cost me to have to write to a woman like that?"

"Like what?" he asked quickly.

"Don't be after asking me what she's like. I wouldn't know.

I never laid eyes on her, nor will I ever if I can help it, please God!"

"But she's his wife!"

"I can call myself the Queen of France, but that doesn't make me one," she retorted. "And how did you dare go through my things? You had no right, Timothy! I don't know what's come over you, I swear to God I don't," she railed at him bitterly. "It's all beyond me. First, all that business of your yearning over those narrowbacks you used to go to see, as though they would care two hoots about you, and now stealing my private letters! I wash my hands of you. I tell you I ought to call in the police, that's what I ought. They send boys to reform school for stealing!"

"Why don't you send me, then?" he sneered. "You'll enjoy hearing what the neighbors say when you walk past them on your way to church!"

They faced each other, their eyes blazing with fury.

The light on the attic stairway was suddenly snapped on.

"For crying out loud, what's going on here?"

Aunt Loretta stood in the doorway in her kimono, blinking at them. Her eyes were puffy with sleep. In spite of his rage at Gran, Timothy couldn't help looking to see if Mary Agnes was there, too. She wasn't. Mary Agnes, he reflected, could sleep through anything.

"You'll have the entire neighborhood at the windows, the two of you!" Aunt Loretta said.

Gran pursed her lips. "Go back to your bed, Loretta!"

"I won't. Not until I know what this is all about."

"It's nothing."

"What do you mean, nothing? The two of you are screaming at each other in the dark, in the middle of the night, and you call it nothing! I thought—My God, I don't know what I thought!"

"Very well," Gran cried. "My grandson is a thief! He's a sneak, a thief, and a liar! I'll never forget what he's done until the day they carry me to my grave. And he'll be the cause That's what he wants! And when I think how I—"

She broke off and stood there shaking with dry sobs. Timothy stared sullenly at the linoleum.

Aunt Loretta drew her hand wearily across her forehead. "For the love of God, Ma, what brought you up here at this time of night, anyway? Go downstairs to bed. We can talk about it tomorrow."

"Tomorrow?" Gran cried feverishly. "We? You keep out of this, Loretta. It's no concern of yours."

"It sure as hell is my concern if it's going to make me miss my beauty sleep and be no good at the Project all day tomorrow! Come downstairs, Ma. You're shaking."

"That's what he's done to me! That's what he's reduced me to! Ah, there's no gratitude in the boy for all the years of loving that I gave him; no respect, Loretta, for my hair that turned gray in taking care of him!"

Aunt Loretta threw a questioning glance at Timothy. "What did you do to your grandmother, anyway?"

"Nothing," he flared. "I only took something that was mine by right."

"Right! By what right?" Gran cried.

And it all began again.

Aunt Loretta finally succeeded in getting Gran to go downstairs. It was not, however, until after other words had been spilled, words so bitter, so angry, and so unreasoning that they burned like acid. And there was no calling those words back anymore.

When he was a little boy, Timothy recalled, and his grandmother came upstairs, he would call out to her after she had kissed him good night, "Ah, Gran, don't leave me alone in the dark!" And she would stay a little longer.

Now, as he lay in the dark again, alone, there was no calling to her to come back. He could only think of the reckless things that she had called out to him in anger and the even more reckless accusations he had hurled back.

There was no calling anything back: not Gran, not the words, not the old trust between them. And then, out of the dark, he gasped at the wild idea that came to his mind, the idea which Mary Agnes had first put words to. The more he thought about it, the more certain he was that he would do it.

He was finished with being only half a person. Nothing would call him back to Duffy's Rocks and this house until he had done it, and found out for himself what he had to know in order to become whole.

And Gran? What about her?

It was her fault, he told himself. She had asked for it. She was the one who had driven him to do it. Besides, he told himself, shivering under the blankets, it was too late to think about Gran or anyone. His mind was set on its course.

TWELVE

Out in It

It was Saturday morning, and Timothy was out in the great world at last.

This time he was really out in it. It was almost impossible for him to believe, but it was actually happening. He was leaving Duffy's Rocks behind, probably forever. He was on his way to New York.

But the great world was not yet rolling past him. He had only taken the first step. He was in the Liberty Avenue bus station, his legs pressed against the small suitcase he had found in the attic. He felt nervously in his inside pocket to make sure that he still had his bus ticket, Mrs. Sevchick's dollar, and Gran's money that he had taken when she was out of the house. He felt a little guilty about that; but it was his, anyway, he told himself. Gran owed it to him for what she had done to him. He made sure, too, that Marjorie's letter was there.

He looked up at the bare face of the clock opposite him. There were still ten minutes before it was time to board the bus.

He sat back and tried to place his thoughts and emotions in some kind of order, but everything was too tangled up for him to sort out. He felt guilt and shame and elation, all mixed up with the fear that Gran would have already realized what he had done and send the police after him before he could get on the bus. He had, too, a breathless feeling of confidence that once he had reached New York he would manage to locate his father. After that, everything would sort itself out, somehow, and be all right. He would find his place in the world. He would be whole: Bart Brennan's son, Timothy Francis Brennan, Esq. He tried to push the panic out of his mind and make plans.

It was hard to make plans when you weren't quite sure what you would find.

He glanced around him at the confusion of people and luggage. On the bench opposite him a couple of sailors sat laughing and blowing out smoke from their cigarettes, their feet propped up on their sea bags, their white caps pushed back on their cropped heads, and their pea jackets flung carelessly open. He wondered where they were going: off to Hawaii, or Naples, or Rio de Janeiro maybe. . . . "Join the Navy and see the world," the posters said. There had been times when he had wished he was old enough to do just that. But now he didn't envy the sailors. Where he was going was enough for him, for the time being.

It was two days since he had found the letter. He tried to block out of his mind the scene in his room at midnight when Gran had learned that he had taken it. The next day had been shrouded in sullen silence. But when he came home from school she had been waiting for him, and a fierce quarrel broke out. He would never be able to forget the things they had said to each other, the scorching words that went on and on and on.

And then, that night, he had packed the bag with his shirts and underwear and hid it in the cellar.

He knew where Gran kept the money for the payments

on the house. He didn't take it all, only as much as he thought he would need to tide him over until he found his father.

He had been worried about getting out of the house with the suitcase, but it was easier than he had thought. Gran was at church. Aunt Loretta was sleeping late. Mary Agnes had been in the bathroom for hours, doing her hair a new way. It was supposed to be a surprise, she said. He had thought about confiding in her, but in the end he had decided not to. She would probably try to come with him, or something.

Even after he boarded the bus and sat back anxiously waiting for it to start, he half-expected to see a policeman arrive to haul him off it. But nothing like that happened. It started on time, and no one came to remove him ignominiously and take him back to Duffy's Rocks.

For a long time he sat with his face pressed to the window watching the world go by. A lot of it didn't seem much different from what he had left behind. The towns they passed through all looked like larger or smaller versions of Duffy's Rocks.

After that he listened to the motherly woman in the seat beside him. She held her flowered hat on her lap, and now and again she bent over it, frowning, to make sure that none of the rigid petals had been disarranged. She informed him that she was going to Harrisburg to visit her married daughter who had just had a baby. He didn't have to talk much. He just told her, when she asked, that he was on his way to New York to visit his father who had a job there. When she asked him where was from, he lied and said Braddock and hoped she didn't know anybody there. She didn't. She did most of the talking, anyway, and after a while she fell asleep with her mouth open, and he sat back and watched the scenery again.

He had decided to spend as little of his money as he could. He didn't know, after all, what lay ahead of him in New York and how much he might really need. So when the bus pulled over beside a refreshment stand for lunch, he just bought a Swiss cheese sandwich and a container of milk. It was a long stop. He was back in the bus long before anyone else, waiting impatiently for it to roll again.

He was relieved when it did.

The sailors, who were sitting in the seat behind him, were laughing and being raucous. Most of the people around them just smiled, but the woman next to him pressed her lips together and shook her head. They offered him a drink from their bottle, but he just said, "No, thank you." After that they lowered their voices. He knew they must be telling dirty jokes. Then, at Harrisburg, the woman got out, leaving her box of pecan crunch. The seat beside him was unoccupied for a while. He ate all the pecan crunch. After that a man got on; he wasn't sure what stop it was because he had been asleep. They didn't talk.

The big bus lumbered steadily across the country. Every time it came to a halt he was afraid a state trooper would come aboard looking for him, but people just got off and others got on, and no one paid any attention to him.

The sailors got out at Philadelphia. A tired-looking woman with two children reeking of Juicy Fruit gum took their place. He was beginning to feel really excited now. He tried to fix on a plan of action for when he reached New York. He didn't know whether to go to Marjorie's address first, or to find a place to stay and then telephone her. Well, he thought, there was still time.

As the bus licked up the miles between Philadelphia and

New York, his elation grew until it was almost unbearable. He had never been so far from Duffy's Rocks in his life. And yet now that he was doing it, it all seemed so easy. He wondered why he hadn't thought of doing it before.

It was dark now, and raining outside. From the way the other passengers began to yank up their ties and reach for their things, he knew they must be nearly there, and he kept his face pressed to the cold window, eager for his first glimpse of the famous skyline. He couldn't make out much, however. Everything was blurry. Then they were going through a tunnel and the bus emerged from it into the brightly lit, rain-streaked streets, and they were there. The aisle was already filled with the other travelers, bumping their way toward the door, anxious to be let out.

Timothy was the last one to get off.

He would have to make up his mind now what to do, he told himself as, bag in hand, he made his way through the confusion of the terminal. A sign said INFORMATION, and he headed toward it.

He showed the address on Marjorie's letter to the man in the information booth, but the man wasn't exactly sure how he could get there. "I live in the Bronx, myself," he said. "The best thing to do is get on the subway to Brooklyn and ask the guy in the change booth, or a guard, or somebody. Just go down the street—that way. You can't miss it. And before you put in your nickel find out if you have to take the IRT or the BMT."

Timothy wasn't sure what the IRT or the BMT was, but he found the subway station easily enough. He had never been in a subway before. It was exhilarating. He was really mingling with the New York crowd, he told himself, as he sniffed the warm stale air and watched the people all around him hurrying to their private destinations. The clicking turnstiles and the rushing roar of the trains underground filled his ears. This was the Symphony of the City!

He was suddenly aware of how tired and hungry he was, and he felt gummy from having spent practically the whole day in the bus. But everything was clear now in his mind. He would go to Brooklyn and find a room somewhere. Then, when he washed and had put on a fresh shirt, he would go and see her. That would be the best thing.

He asked a guard how to get to Marjorie's address. The guard told him which train to take and where to get out.

As he dropped his nickel into the slot and passed through the turnstile, he felt as though he was really in New York.

The subway train was crowded. There was no place to sit, and it wasn't easy to peer out of the window at the names of the stations. He began to get nervous, afraid that he would miss his stop.

But then he saw the name of the station hanging over the platform, and he squeezed his way out of the car, and made his way up to the street.

The street he emerged onto was very different from the area around the bus terminal. The traffic was much quieter, and there weren't any of the garish electric signs to be seen. The rain was a chilly drizzle now. He stood hesitantly, looking up at the street sign on the corner.

A passing policeman stopped and looked at him.

A sudden panic filled Timothy. Was the alarm out for him already? Gran must have gotten in touch with the Missing Persons Bureau. He thought of running, but he didn't know which way to run.

The policeman came up to him.

"What are you looking for, sonny?" he asked. "Can I help you?"

Timothy bit back a sigh of relief.

He said, "I was just looking for a place to stay."

The policeman said, "There's a YMCA." He jerked his thumb over his shoulder. "That's five blocks over that way." He considered. "Or, there's the Carroll Hotel, if you want. It's just down the street—clean and cheap and nice."

"Thanks," Timothy said.

He decided that he would try the hotel.

He went along the street, past a row of identical brownstone houses until he saw the sign: CARROLL HOTEL: TRANSIENT AND WEEKLY RATES. It wasn't at all like the William Penn. It seemed to have been formed by the knocking together of a couple of old brownstone fronts. He peered through the window at the lobby. It was shabby, with faded artificial flowers in dusty glass vases and worn leather chairs. But, as the policeman had said, it was clean.

There was a young man with an old face behind the desk.

"I'm looking for a room," Timothy said timidly.

The desk clerk eyed him and his bag.

Then Timothy remembered Mary Agnes' admiring glance at him in the William Penn Hotel. She had said that he looked like some rich kid from out of town. He said quickly, "My father is due in from the West and I'm supposed to wait for him until he gets here." He was astonished at how smoothly the lie rolled from his lips.

The man nodded. "I guess we can fix you up," he said.

"How much is it?"

The man told him. It was a lot cheaper by the week.

Timothy reflected, making some rapid calculations. Then

he said, "I might as well take it for a week. I'm not sure exactly what day my dad's getting here. Do I have to pay now?"

The man's pale eyes lingered on Timothy's old suitcase.

"By the week," he said, "payment is always in advance."

Timothy paid, thinking that if he was careful the money that was left ought to last him until he found his father.

The room clerk pushed a big book toward him. "Just sign the register, please," he said.

"T. F. Brady," Timothy wrote. Brady was his grandmother's maiden name. Where it said ADDRESS he put the street number of the Lachlans' house in Shadyside.

The clerk hardly glanced at it. He ran his fingers along a row of cubby holes behind him and took down a key with a heavy metal tab on it.

"It's room 12," he said. "Up one flight. Bathroom's down the hall."

Room 12 was clean, even if it was rather bare. It held a single bed, a night table with a Bible on it, a floor lamp, a rather saggy chair, a chest of drawers, and a sink with a streaked mirror over it. There was a notice pasted on the mirror. It said that guests were requested to be sure to turn off the faucet after using the hot water, and that cooking and ironing were not allowed in the rooms. For two-day laundry service, inquire at the desk. The window looked out onto a dark courtyard.

Timothy unpacked his few things. He washed up and put on a clean shirt and his good suit. Then he went downstairs. He was hungry. The clerk told him, when he asked, that there was a Waldorf Cafeteria in the next street.

Before he went and ate, however, he decided that he would find the house where his father's wife lived. He didn't know why. He just wanted to look at it.

He found it easily. It was only four short blocks from Carroll. It was a four-story brownstone building, with four bells and name slots on the door frame, from which he assumed that it was divided into four apartments. From the position of the bell with BRENNAN under it, he understood that she lived on the second floor. He glanced up at the windows. The shades were pulled down, but there was a glow of light behind them, which meant that she was home.

He was tempted to ring the bell. All he had to do was to stretch out his finger and push the little button and he would know what she looked like. Maybe she was having her supper now. Perhaps she would ask him to join her, and they would have a cozy supper together and after that a long chat about his father.

Then he decided that he couldn't just go barging in on her while she was eating. She was his father's wife, but she was a stranger to him. He decided to wait. Then, if she was having her supper when he went to see her, he could say politely that he had already eaten, thank you.

The cafeteria was all right, even though it wasn't what he had really dreamed of as the setting for his first dinner in New York. It didn't matter, he told himself. After he found his father it would all be different.

He had baked beans and apple pie. They were the cheapest. They were also the most filling things they had. He couldn't imagine why just sitting in the bus all day could have made him so hungry.

He sat at his table for a while looking around him at the people. He was astonished that, even though they were New Yorkers, they weren't all that different, to look at, from the people at home. They didn't look at all sophisticated: just tired and ordinary.

Then he went to the men's room. He washed his hands and face carefully. He wet his hair and slicked it back as best he could. Looking at himself in the mirror he wondered what his father's wife would think of him. He hoped he looked enough like his father for her to like him.

After that, he went out into the street again and walked quickly over to the house. It occurred to him that perhaps she had gone out in the meantime. Surely, everyone in New York went out on Saturday night. But no, the lights were still on.

His heart pounding, he ran up the steps and pressed his finger to the bell with the name Brennan on it.

THIRTEEN

Marjorie

Timothy held his breath and waited.

After a moment the buzzer on the front door began clicking.

He pushed the door open. He found himself in a long hallway covered with dim brown wallpaper. It held a long table with letters scattered on it, presumably for the tenants. A waist-high Japanese jar stood in the corner, filled with dried-out pampas grass.

There was a mirror on one wall. He adjusted his tie in the mottled glass. He looked all right, he guessed.

Then he heard a woman's voice calling down to him, "Who is it?"

He cleared his throat.

"Mrs. Brennan?"

"Yes. Who is it?"

He couldn't make her out in the meager light.

He called up to her, "Could I just see you for a minute?"

The woman emerged onto the landing above him and leaned over the banister.

"What do you want?" she asked. "I'm sick and tired of people ringing my bell and asking for contributions."

She stood there, unsmiling, watching him while he climbed the stairs.

Timothy wasn't at all sure what he expected his father's second wife to be like. He had merely supposed that she would probably be as beautiful as his own mother was in her pictures—only not wearing those old-fashioned clothes, of course.

He was not, however, prepared to see, when he reached the landing, this small, neat, worn-looking woman with a thin face and faded hair set in stiff waves. She had on a dark dress and no jewelry except for a thin, white-gold wedding band on her left hand.

"Mrs. Brennan?" he asked uncertainly as he stood in front of her. He was probably, he told himself, on the wrong floor. "Are you Mrs. Marjorie Brennan?"

She nodded.

He mustered up an uneasy smile.

"All right. Well?" she demanded.

He said, swallowing, "I'm Timothy."

"Timothy?" She repeated the name blankly.

Then she peered at him and let out a small gasp.

"Oh, my God!" she exclaimed, running her hand over her hair. "You must be his son!"

He nodded silently and waited.

She pressed her lips together. "Well," she told him, "I guess you had better come inside."

As he followed her into the apartment he had a blurred impression of a modestly furnished living room. The radio was going, turned on to a news program. On the low cigarette-scarred table in front of the couch there was a half-empty coffee cup.

She walked over to the radio and switched it off.

"You might as well sit down," she said, picking the afternoon paper, folded at the unfinished crossword, off the easy chair.

He sat down. He felt an odd sensation as he did so. He knew that it must be his father's chair.

She lowered herself onto the couch. She looked pale and disconcerted.

"Well?" she said harshly.

He smiled nervously at her. Through the half-opened kitchen door he had caught a glimpse of unwashed dishes stacked in the sink. And there were touches of neglect in the living room, as though the person who lived there no longer cared very much how things looked.

"What are you doing here?" she asked, her voice still harsh. "I thought you were living in Duffy's Rocks with your grandmother."

"I was," he told her. "Until today."

The glance she gave him was as sharp as a knife, tipped with suspicion.

"What did she send you here for?" she demanded.

The question confused him. "Who?" he asked.

"Your grandmother," she snapped impatiently. "Who else?"

"She didn't send me," he said.

"Oh, she didn't? You just decided to come, and broke your piggy bank, and here you are?"

He said, with as much dignity as he could, "My grandmother doesn't even know that I'm here in New York."

She patted her hair and looked incredulous. "She doesn't?"

"No. I just came on my own."

"Look," she said. "Whether your grandmother sent you or not doesn't really make any difference to me. Let me just make one thing absolutely clear to you before we go any further."

He stared at her, picking furtively at an old scab on one of his knuckles.

"Yes?" he said.

"It's this: he isn't here."

"I know," he said.

"Then what—"

"I found your letter to my grandmother. That's why I decided to come and see you."

Her expression of suspicion and defensiveness turned to one of perplexity. She pressed a hand against her forehead.

"I don't think I understand what you're trying to say," she said.

"It's like this, Mrs. Brennan—" This time he stumbled over the name.

She cut in, saying, "I guess you might as well call me Marjorie." She permitted her lips to curl briefly into a wan smile. "Mrs. Brennan sounds rather peculiar coming from his son."

He wanted to explain, to tell her the whole story from the beginning. But she might misunderstand. And it was difficult for him to speak with her sitting opposite him, her knees pressed rigidly together, her hands clasped in her lap, and her eyes boring right into his. He could see now that, even with her long nose and sallow complexion, she must have been a pretty woman once. It was just the tiredness and tightness in her face that made her look so pinched and middle-aged.

She bent stiffly forward. "All right. Tell me, what did you come here to see me for, Timothy?" She hesitated slightly before speaking his name. Her voice was somewhat less harsh now.

He had resumed picking at the scab on his knuckle. He stopped now, and the words came out in a nervous rush. "I came to New York by myself on the bus," he said. "I came because I want to find my father. It's something personal I have to see him about. I thought," he finished lamely, "that you might be able to help me."

"Help you?" she said. "But how? You say you read my answer to your grandmother's letter. So you know that I have no idea where he is." She reached for a cigarette, tapped the end of it on her wrist, and lit it. Her hands were trembling slightly. "What's more, I'm not even sure I want to know where he is."

She blew a thin steam of smoke up toward the ceiling, while he stared helplessly at her.

"Don't you even know where he went?" he asked.

She shrugged her thin shoulders again.

"I just came home from the office one evening and put the dinner in the oven and waited for him, but he never showed up. Then I looked around, in the closet, and I saw that his things were gone."

Timothy's eyes traveled around the room. It was hard to think that his father had lived in this apartment for so long and that there was now no trace of him in it. He was sitting in his father's chair but it was just a chair like any other, the upholstery threadbare at the armrests. It was as though his father had never sat in it.

"Didn't he leave a letter behind, or anything?"

"He was never one for leaving letters," she said.

She lit another cigarette. "Oh, it wasn't such a shock as you might think," she resumed. "It wasn't the first time he got restless and threw up his job and went off."

"What happened those other times?" he asked.

"He always came back after a few days, saying he'd been to Boston or Philly or I don't know where. Once he stayed away for over three weeks. He'd gone out to California, he said, that time. He went looking for something better. That's what he said, every damned time. And even though anyone in her right mind would have known the only thing to do would have been to call it quits, I always took him back, every damned time. Oh, he knows how to cajole and get around a person. 'Come on, Marjorie, don't be like that! You know what I'm like. . . .'" She let out a hard, dry laugh. "Trust his Irish charm for that. Yes, I knew what he's like. Even so, if he were to turn the key in the front door and walk in here right now and give me that boyish grin of his, after leaving me alone for over a year without a word of news, not even a postcard to say he was still alive and grinning, I suppose I'd tell him to hang up his hat and put his feet up while I fixed him something he liked—even though my common sense would tell me to slam the door in his face."

"Did you call up the place where he worked?" Timothy persisted.

"The Briggs Company, you mean?"

He nodded.

"As a matter of fact, after a few days of waiting, I managed to swallow what was left of my pride, and I called his office. They told me he hadn't shown up in over a week. They were fed up. A business isn't a woman. It won't sit around and wait for a man to come back. They'd already replaced him."

"But—" he began.

"Look," she said. "Forget him. I know he's your father, and you're at the age when a boy needs a man to look up to. But what did he ever do for you? Or for anyone who loved him? I'm doing my best to forget him. Fortunately, I have my job—not that it's terribly thrilling, but it always paid the rent and the bills when he was between jobs, which was most of the time." She looked at him through narrowed eyes. "If you want my advice, you'll go scuttling back to Duffy's Rocks where you belong." She reached for her purse. "You probably need some money to get back," she said.

"I have enough," he told her. He got up. "I guess I ought to go now. I'm sorry I bothered you."

She said, "Where will you go?"

"I don't know. I'm going to try to find him, I guess. That's what I came for."

"Where?" she asked. "How?"

"I don't know," he confessed.

"He may not even be in New York."

He nodded.

"And even if he is, it's a big city. Over six million people live here."

"I know," he said.

"'Go and catch a falling star,'" she muttered between her teeth.

He looked inquiringly at her.

"Don't mind me," she said. "I was just quoting something. Forget what I said." She fell silent, staring at the wall. Then she turned her heavy eyes toward him and shaped her lips into a wry smile. "I hope that you find him, for your sake," she said.

"I will," he told her confidently.

"Good luck," she said. "And if you do—"

"Yes?"

"Nothing."

"Look," he said. "Is there anything you want me to tell him for you when I find him?"

She closed her eyes for a moment. "No," she said at last. "I have nothing to tell him."

"I'll say good-bye, then," Timothy said.

She stubbed out her cigarette and began to light another. She did not answer.

Timothy let himself out, closing the door on her silence. Then he walked down the dim stairs and into the dark, empty street.

FOURTEEN

Skyline

The drizzle had stopped. The streets of Brooklyn were shiny now.

Timothy stood in front of Marjorie's house wondering where to go. He turned over in his mind the idea of riding back to New York on the subway to explore the famous bright lights. He found that he had no taste for them now.

Instead, he walked around the neighborhood, getting what comfort he could from the thought that these were the streets his father had walked every day. It was a section of old, established homes, a few of which had been turned into apartments, like the one in which Marjorie lived. He liked their solidity. Whenever he came upon a house where the shades were not lowered he peered through the curtains, staring at the lamplit rooms, and envying the people who lived in them. Sometimes he even caught a glimpse of someone sitting reading, or of a group talking around a table. There seemed to be a party going on in one of the houses. Men and women in evening dress were making their way up the steps to the front door. He watched them until one of the group turned and caught his eye. Then he moved on, guiltily.

A few blocks after that he found himself on a business

street, clogged with the Saturday night crowds. It had big department stores, like downtown at home, and theatres and restaurants. There was a Childs', where a pretty red-haired waitress flipped over griddle cakes as she made them right there in the window. He watched her until she looked out and smiled at him. He smiled back. A few men stood listlessly on the corners. They had crates with piles of red apples and hand-lettered signs saying, Unemplyed. Buy an Apple Only 5¢. Timothy waited to see if any people stopped to buy them. Not many did.

It was still too early to go back to the room at the Carroll Hotel. There was nothing to do there but sleep. He was tired, but he wasn't sleepy yet. He kept on walking.

Eventually, he found himself in front of a large building. It was brightly lit up inside. It was a public library, and it was open.

He trudged up the steps and through the doors.

A librarian looked up from behind the jar of dried flowers on her desk and asked in a whisper if she could help him find anything.

He said, "No, thank you. I'd just like to look around."

He pulled out a few books at random and glanced at them. Then he gravitated toward the section where the newspapers hung from their racks. The New York papers were much thicker than the ones at home. He took one over to a table and leafed through it. He was astonished at the long list of plays and concerts: all those famous names, and all in person, not just movies! It would be difficult to decide which one to go to—that was, if you had the money. There was so much to do in New York—in the world, for that matter—if you only had the money.

Suddenly, Timothy didn't feel like reading anymore.

He went out of the library and began walking again, taking every green light and seeing where it would lead him. He found himself in a network of narrow streets. And then, without warning, when he turned a corner, he was out on a long promenade overlooking a river. Overhead, a dark bridge spanned the sky. He could detect the small lights of automobiles crossing it. It was the bridge to Manhattan. Across the river, there was the city's nighttime skyline with its thrusting skyscrapers and their lighted windows. The sight made his heart leap into his throat.

He stood there for a long time, gazing at it. Somewhere in it all, he was sure, was his father: the one person he had come here to find, without whom the city had no meaning.

All those buildings, all those windows—would he ever find him there?

As he watched, a star fell in the sky behind the mass of granite.

Go and catch a falling star! That was what Marjorie had said. How, he wondered, could he ever catch it? His eyes followed it until it disappeared, falling—who could tell where?—into the city's population of over six million.

A feeling of overwhelming tiredness swept over him. He had left Duffy's Rocks only that morning, but already it seemed far away. It seemed a whole lifetime away.

He turned and made his way back to the hotel. His feet were heavy, as though his shoes had soles of iron, and he had to ask for directions several times before he found it. The lobby was empty, smelling of stale cigar smoke and Lysol.

He climbed the shabby stairs to Room 12.

FIFTEEN

The Sidewalks of New York

Timothy awoke with the gray sunlight from the courtyard in his eyes.

It took him a long moment to realize where he was and remember why he was there.

He got out of bed and went over to the window. There was nothing to see, only other windows. There was no sign of life anywhere except for a cat on a fire escape, licking itself in the thin warmth. Timothy thought of Mr. Kinsella. This cat didn't look as sleek.

Sunday morning quiet hung over everything. Timothy wondered what Marjorie, a few blocks away, was doing. Perhaps she was still asleep, but he imagined her sitting in the kitchen jabbing endless cigarettes into her empty coffee cup and doing the Sunday crossword puzzle. He speculated as to whether there would be any sense in trying to see her again. He could telephone her first, this time. But he was sure that it wouldn't do any good. He had learned yesterday all that Marjorie had to tell him.

He dressed and went downstairs. Some elderly men were sitting around the lobby. They looked up at him, briefly curious, and then glanced away. The desk clerk said, "Good morning, Mr. Brady," and it was a moment before Timothy recollected that Mr. Brady was himself. He stammered "Good morning" back and did his best to saunter over to the front door, feeling slightly self-conscious, aware that the elderly men and the desk clerk were all looking in his direction.

In the street, everything looked different in the daylight. The cafeteria was open and he had his breakfast there, at a table by the window. He debated with himself as to whether he would go back to the place overlooking the river. He wanted to see the New York skyline by day. Well, there would be time for that later.

Then he had an idea.

He went over to the telephone booth. It dismayed him a little to discover that there were five directories, not counting the Classified, all for New York City and all of them incredibly thick.

He was sure it wouldn't do any good, but he had to start somewhere. He looked in every one of them—Manhattan, Brooklyn, Staten Island, Queens, and the Bronx, under the name "Brennan." It seemed to him that there were more Brennans in New York then there could be in the whole of Ireland! But the only Bartholomew he found was a Bartholomew R., in the Bronx. There wouldn't be any sense trying that one: his father's name didn't have a middle initial. There were, however, a number of plain Brennan, B.'s. For one wild instant he considered trying them all in the chance that one of them might turn out to be the right one. But he dismissed the thought. He didn't have enough money to throw away that many nickels.

He would have to think of something else.

He opened the Manhattan book again and found the Briggs Company. It was on East Fortieth Street. He wrote the address on the back of the envelope which contained Marjorie's letter.

After that he went down into the subway and rode to Manhattan.

With some difficulty he found the building where the Briggs Company had its offices. It was a skyscraper. Although not one of the very biggest, it was still impressive. It was right on Fifth Avenue, near the Public Library. The front doors were locked because it was Sunday, but it was still a satisfaction to him just to be able to look at it.

Then he walked back to the Public Library with its two great stone lions that gazed out onto the Avenue. He scanned all the faces that passed thinking that, after all, a miracle might happen. He might just bump into his father by chance, the way it happened in books.

"Dad!"

"Timothy! What brings you here, to Fifth Avenue of all places?"

"I was looking for you, Dad. They say that if you stand on the corner of Fifth Avenue and Forty-Second Street, eventually the whole world goes by. That's what I read somewhere."

But none of the faces was his father's.

After a long while he moved on. Maybe, he thought ruefully, he hadn't stood there long enough.

Suddenly, he found himself in front of a great gray church which took up a whole block. He knew that it must be St. Patrick's Cathedral.

He went inside and stood until his eyes grew used to the darkness. Mass was coming to an end. He slipped as unobtrusively as he could into a seat at the back and listened to the Latin words being intoned at the altar. It was as familiar as St. Bridget's, and yet it was so different, filling him with happy awe. This was what the cathedrals in Europe must be like. He lifted his eyes up to the seemingly limitless vaulted ceiling and said a quick prayer under his breath. Maybe, he thought, it would mean more in a church like this.

When he went out again the sun was high and the Avenue was full of people. Soon he forgot why he was there in New York and lost himself in the excitement of merely being there.

That day Timothy wandered all over Manhattan. The shop windows were much more sumptuous than the ones in Pittsburgh. Some of them were even lighted like sets for a play. He ate in the Automat, which was a glorious adventure. He walked all the way from Times Square to Battery Park. He was Stanley and Balboa and Cortes and Richard Halliburton and all the explorers he had ever read about. Everywhere there was something that was strange and new to him; or else something he knew about already, which was exciting to see because it was the real thing, not just a picture in a book. He longed to belong to it all, to be part of it. He could not imagine how he could ever go back to the colorless streets of Duffy's Rocks after the sidewalks of New York.

It was dark when he finally rode the subway back to Brooklyn.

He was tempted to try some new place for his supper, but he was cautious of his remaining money. The Waldorf Cafeteria was cheap and the portions were large, so he went there. When he returned to the hotel he was grateful for the familiar bare room. His feet ached. His mind ached too with remembering and sorting out everything he had seen.

He undressed and stretched out on the bed. He fell asleep almost at once. The wonders of New York sailed through the sea of his dreams, tumbling over each other and recurring like a school of endless dolphins.

Timothy had meant to get up early the next day but he overslept. The morning was already half gone when he finally pushed through the subway turnstile on his way back to Manhattan.

This time he found the skyscraper on the East Fortieth Street easily. The directory in the teeming lobby informed him that the offices of Briggs Company were on the eighteenth floor.

The girl behind the switchboard at the reception desk was young and pretty. He stood apprehensively at the little window and waited while she put through several calls. Finally, she looked up at him.

He swallowed. "I wanted to ask about somebody who used to work here," he said.

"What name?"

"Brennan," he told her. "Bartholomew Brennan."

"Could you wait a minute, please?" She put another call through the board. Then she turned to him. "Brennan?" She knit her brows. "There's nobody here named that."

"I said he used to work here," he reminded her shyly.

"Oh. Well, I'm new here. Let me just ask around." She plugged in a wire. "Eleanor?" she said into the mouthpiece. "Listen, there's a boy out here looking for someone named Brennan. Ever hear of him? . . . Oh . . . Well, go ahead and ask Mrs. Pearson. I'll hold . . . What? . . . All right, I'll tell him." She pulled out the cord and turned back to Timothy. "He left over a year ago," she said.

"I know."

"He used to be in the drafting department, with Mr. Frank."

He swallowed again. "Could I— Could I speak to Mr. Frank, maybe? I wouldn't keep him long. Could you just ask him, please?"

She said cheerfully, "It can't hurt to ask." She got up. "Just come through that door and wait here. I'll be right back. What name shall I tell Mr. Frank?"

"Brennan," he said.

He stared around the reception room while she was gone. There wasn't much to see. And there weren't any windows to look out of and see the city spread out below the eighteenth floor, as he had hoped.

She was back. "Mr. Frank'll see you," she said. "Go through that door, past the water cooler. He's the last on the left."

He wanted to thank her but the switchboard was buzzing again.

He went through the corridor. There were cubicles on either side, where men in shirtsleeves worked at drawing boards or leaned over spread-out blueprints. In the last cubicle on the left a heavy-set man with glasses sat behind a desk.

Timothy hesitated in the doorway before rapping discreetly on its frame.

"Come right in, Bart. What brings you here?" Then Mr. Frank looked up. "Who the hell are you?"

"I'm Timothy Brennan," he said. "I'm Bart's son."

"Oh," Mr. Frank said. "It's the first time I heard that he had a—" he broke off, scratched his head, pushed his glasses up onto his forehead, and pointed to a chair near his desk. "Well, come in and take a pew."

Timothy carefully sat down.

"What can I do for you, Mr. Brennan?" The heavy man grinned. "Not looking for a job, are you?"

Timothy shook his head.

Mr. Frank laughed. "Practically everyone else who comes to see me is," he said. "I get tired of telling them all there's nothing." He swung around in his chair. "How's your old man getting on?"

Timothy gulped. "I don't know," he said. "That's what I came to see you about." He paused. Then he added, "Sir."

"Me? But how would I know? Your father threw up his job here, let me see— Oh, some time ago. I don't remember when it was."

"I know that, sir," Timothy said.

"Then what's the—?" Mr. Frank broke off and tilted his chair backwards. "What was your name, son?" he asked.

"Timothy," he said.

"All right, Timothy. Now tell me what brings you here."

Timothy looked down at his hands in embarrassment. He would probably get sick of telling people why he was there, he thought, before his search ended.

"Go ahead," Mr. Frank urged. "It's probably not easy. Just say the words."

And so, doggedly, Timothy told Mr. Frank that he had come from Duffy's Rocks looking for his father; that his father's second wife had had no word from him in over a year; and that he had thought of trying his father's old office to see if they had any idea as to where he might be now. "And I guess that's it," he said.

Mr. Frank nodded thoughtfully. "Well, personally, I wouldn't know where to find him. But then I never saw him much after office hours. Oh, we'd have lunch together sometimes with a gang of others, if you know what I mean. But I never went to his house or met his wife. As a matter of fact, I didn't know he'd been married before. So I don't think I'm the man to help you."

Timothy had a sinking feeling in the pit of his stomach. It didn't look as though anyone could help him.

Mr. Frank frowned. "Let me try the personnel office and see if anyone there knows anything," he said, picking up the telephone. The person he spoke to, however, said they had no information as to where Bartholomew Brennan had gone when he left the company, and no forwarding address. There had been no request for a reference, or if there had been, they had no record of it.

Mr. Frank hung up and spread his hands out on the desk. "And that's it," he said, shrugging his massive shoulders. "Draughtsmen come and go all the time. We can't keep track of them all. There's nothing else I can do for you, son. I'm sorry."

"Thank you, anyway," Timothy said dully. He should have known that it wouldn't be any good. It had all seemed too easy. He wondered where he could possibly go from here. "I'm sorry that I bothered you."

Mr. Frank stood up and gave Timothy a clumsy pat. "Don't you worry, son," he said. "I'm sure you'll find your father. If you were my boy, and I'd lost track of you, so to speak, I know damned well I'd want you to come and find me."

Timothy was still reluctant to leave. He said, "Isn't there anywhere else I could go and ask?"

Mr. Frank furrowed his forehead. He didn't say anything for a long time. Then, "There is somebody," he said slowly. He got up. "You just wait here a minute, son. Don't go away while I dash over to the personnel office. There's something I just remembered and it might just—"

Before he could finish the sentence, Mr. Frank vanished through the doorway.

After a while he came back. "Well," he said, "this isn't much. It's the name and number of someone who used to work here, someone who just might have some idea where he went." He handed Timothy a folded pink sheet torn from an office memo pad.

Timothy shoved it into his pocket. Anyway, it was a ray of hope.

"I hope it isn't a wild-goose chase," Mr. Frank said. "Anyway," he added apologetically, "it's the best I could do."

He watched from the doorway of his cubicle, scratching his head gently, as Timothy walked away down the corridor.

It was not until he reached the lobby of the building that Timothy took the memo out of his pocket. "Frieda Blaufeld," he read. And under the name Mr. Frank had scrawled a telephone number, and an address somewhere in Queens.

SIXTEEN

The End
of the Line

Timothy lost no time in finding a telephone booth and dialing the number. He wasn't sure what he was going to say when the person spoke at the other end. He would think of something when the ringing stopped.

He waited while it rang a dozen times. No one answered.

He spent the afternoon wandering around the streets, looking at everything and not seeing anything in particular. Every half hour or so he tried the number again. Each time there was no reply.

Perhaps, he thought, Frieda Blaufeld worked during the day. He was tired of walking. The rush hour had begun, flooding the streets with people who brushed by without even looking at him. He was ready to go down into the subway and go back to the hotel. Then he decided to try just once more.

At the third ring someone picked up the telephone.

"Yes?" a woman said.

He asked, a little breathlessly, "Could I please speak to Frieda Blaufeld?"

"Frieda is not here." It was a voice with a heavy accent—German, he guessed.

"Please," he persisted. "Could I speak to her just for a minute?" He added, "It's important."

There was no answer. For a moment he thought that she had hung up, or that the line had gone dead. But at last she said, "If you try maybe after seven o'clock, I think she will be home." Then she hung up.

He went back to Brooklyn, to the hotel. There was nothing else to do. He lay on the bed waiting for seven o'clock. Then he got restless and went downstairs. He sat in the lobby where there was a clock over the reception desk.

At five minutes to seven he dialed the number again.

A different voice answered this time. It was softer than the other, and it too had a German accent, although a much fainter one.

"This is Frieda Blaufeld speaking. Who is it, please?"

He managed to blurt out his name.

There was a moment's silence.

"Who, please?"

He repeated it. "I'm Bartholomew Brennan's son," he added lamely.

There was a stifled sound, like a gasp, in the receiver.

He waited.

"Where did you get my name?" she finally asked in a low voice.

"From the Briggs Company," he said. "From Mr. Frank. He mentioned you knew my father."

"I see."

He went on in a rush, "I wondered if maybe I could see you and ask you a few questions about my father."

She said, after a long pause, "If you like. Why not?"

"When?"

"I'm home tonight. Could you come out here?"

"Yes, Miss Blaufeld. I would like to do that if it's all right with you," he said.

"Do you know Queens?"

He told her that he had never been there.

"I see. Well, if you tell me where you are and when you will start, I will meet you at the station."

He told her where he was, adding that he would leave right away.

She let him know which subway train to take and where to change. "Then you ride to the end of the line. I will meet you at the far end of the platform, where you get out."

He hesitated. "But how will we recognize each other?"

"I will wear a yellow scarf on my head. And you? What do you look like? Never mind. If you are Bart's boy I will know you right away."

Getting there was rather easy, really. He sat in the half empty subway car thinking about her. Who could she be, this German woman? What did she have to do with his father? And would she know where Bart Brennan was?

When the train came to a final halt, the station platform was almost empty.

Then he caught sight of her. She was standing right near the exit. He knew her at once from the yellow scarf with the blue flowers printed on it, and from the look on her face.

SEVENTEEN

The Way
of the Wind

He passed through the turnstile.

She was younger than Marjorie, with fresh high color in her cheeks and short dark hair which curled out from under her yellow scarf. She had on a dark skirt and white blouse and low-heeled shoes. A heavy sweater was flung over her shoulders.

She held out her hand. She said, "It didn't take you long to get here, did it?"

He said, "The train was fast, I guess."

She nodded. "It was the express train."

They stood there awkwardly, looking at each other and not knowing what to say.

Then, "We can't stand here all night, in the subway!" she exclaimed. She started up the stairs. He followed her. They emerged into a quiet neighborhood of small stores and trees and little bungalows with neat patches of grass in front of each.

"It's not far from here," she said. They went on for several blocks, each one very much like the one before it. Finally, she halted in front of a two-story brick house in a row of others just like it. "This is where I live."

She unlocked the front door. Then she unlocked another door which opened into a flight of steep stairs.

The apartment, what he could see of it, was small. The lamps were all lit. There wasn't much furniture, but everything was spotless, and there was a pot of flowers on the window sill. When they came in, a thin pale woman who looked older than Frieda got up from where she sat.

"This is my sister Trudi," Miss Blaufeld said. "Trudi, this is Bart's son. Did you ever imagine Bart could already have such a big boy?"

"Good evening," Trudi said without smiling. When she spoke, he realized that it was she to whom he had first spoken.

The two sisters exchanged a glance. Then Frieda said something in a low tone, in what Timothy assumed was German.

Trudi went into another room. A moment later she came out wearing her coat and hat. "I was just going out," she explained. "Good-bye," she said to Timothy. "It was very nice to meet you."

They were alone.

As Timothy stood in the middle of the room wondering what to say, Frieda Blaufeld looked at him. "Did you have supper?" she asked.

He shook his head. "I forgot to."

She laughed. "That's very unusual," she said. "I didn't think boys ever forgot to eat. Sit down here, I'll make you something. We will talk later."

He sat down at the table by the window and looked around the room while she moved about in the kitchen. His eye lit on an enlarged snapshot of a man and woman feeding pigeons in a park. They looked very happy. With a small shock he realized that it was his father and Frieda Blaufeld.

He was still staring at it when she came back into the room with a tablecloth. He looked guiltily away.

She only said, "Yes, that was with your father. It was taken about a year ago."

She set the table for him.

"You shouldn't go to so much trouble just for me," he told her.

"But it is no trouble!" she answered. "Your father always said I had a passion for feeding people. Only there is not very much in the refrigerator." She looked rueful. "If I had known!"

While he ate, she sat across from him and watched. Ordinarily he would have felt self-conscious, sitting in a strange apartment with a woman he had just met who anxiously watched every mouthful that he put to his lips. But it seemed natural enough with her. There was an omelette crisp on the outside and runny on the inside, and black bread, which astonished him; it was just like the bread in Mrs. Sevchick's house. And there was cheesecake. He had never tasted cheesecake before.

He ate everything, down to the cheesecake's last crumb.

"Was it enough?" she asked, bringing him a glass of milk.

"Oh, yes," he said.

"You are sure?" she insisted doubtfully.

"It was more than enough," he assured her. "And every thing was very delicious, thank you."

He sat back in his chair, crossed his legs, and rested his arms on the sides of the chair, letting his hands hang down.

She stared at him, wide-eyed.

"What's the matter?" he asked uneasily. "Is anything wrong?"

"No," she said, with an effort. "It's nothing. It's only that you are sitting in that chair exactly the way your father used to sit after a meal." She paused. "And when you speak, I have the same feeling. You talk just like Bart."

"Do I?" he asked, pleased.

She nodded gravely. Then she said, "Bart never— You know, I never knew before that he had a son."

"Didn't you ever ask him?" Timothy asked. "I mean, about the past, about the time before—" He broke off, not knowing how to finish.

She shook her head. "I don't know if you can understand this," she said. "But we were so happy living in the present. And any time I mentioned something about his years before he knew me, it was like a cloud over us. So I didn't ask anymore. Now that you are here, it all seems— Oh, I don't know. I think that I am a little confused about it still." She leaned forward and smiled at him. "Anyway, I am glad you came. Now, what can I tell you?"

Timothy swallowed.

Then the words came out. "Where is he?"

She didn't answer at once. Then she said, "But, Timothy, you came too late. He is gone."

He was seized with sudden apprehension.

"Gone?"

"He left a month ago."

A month ago! His heart pounded. So close! If he had come to New York a month ago–

"You can tell me where he went, though, can't you? So that I can find him?"

"You won't find him. He went to Mexico."

He repeated blankly, "Mexico?"

"I think, Mexico. Or he might have ended up in Guatemala."

His eyes were fixed on the tablecloth and the empty dishes in front of him, and the glass still coated with the milk he had drunk from it, without seeing any of it.

"He had been talking about going for months," she said. "He was fed up, he said, with New York. I tried to keep him here, but I could not hold him. Nothing could hold Bart when he was in that mood. I think that you did not know your father very well, so let me tell you this. He was always, since I knew him, I don't know—" She groped for the words. "Restless? Forever running away from reality?" She turned her head toward the window. "I only know that if you love someone, you love him for what he is. If you try to change him, it is a terrible risk because then you are in danger of changing what you love."

"But you must have heard from him since he left?" Timothy persisted.

"No." She paused. She said, "He wanted me to go with him."

"Why didn't you?"

Her eyes were still on the dark windowpane. There was a long silence before she replied. "We had been happy together. But how could I believe in his wild, restless schemes anymore?"

Timothy was only half listening to her. He was thinking that every small step he took toward his father only brought him to a place where he found that his father had taken another giant step further away into the unknown. Wherever Bart Brennan went—New York, California, Mexico, or even as far as the Land of the Peacock Throne, it would only be to leave again on the way of the wind to find some other place where his past life would never catch up with him.

After that she asked Timothy about himself, about where he lived, about his grandmother. She really seemed to want to know, but it was hard to answer. He no longer felt like talking.

She said, "I will walk with you to the subway."

They went back through the quiet streets. Most of the houses were already dark.

At the subway station she looked anxiously into his face. "What will you do now?"

"I don't know," he said.

"Will you come to see me again, Timothy," she asked, "before you go home?"

He said he would. He knew as he said it that he probably wouldn't.

"Please call me at least," she said. She held something out in her hand. "And please let me give you this."

It was money.

He drew back. "I couldn't take it," he said.

"But it is only a present for your next birthday."

He shook his head.

"Please," she begged. "Consider that it comes from Bart. He would want you to have it."

He took it and put it in his pocket without looking at it. "Thank you," he said. He shifted his feet. "I have to go now."

"Do you know what train to take?"

"Yes," he said.

She said, "Well, Timothy—"

Then, suddenly, she bent and kissed him on the cheek. "That was from your father, too," she said.

He did not say anything.

"I am glad that you came," she said.

When he was downstairs, on the station platform, waiting for the train, he looked at what she had given him. It was a worn ten-dollar bill.

The train roared in. He stared at the faces that came at him through the doors. "Get out of my way!" he raged at them under his breath. "I want to see my father."

EIGHTEEN

A Bench
in the Park

Timothy woke the next morning to stare dully at the bare walls and the soot-streaked window of the drab hotel that held him. He thought for a while of getting up and going out, but he didn't feel like going anywhere. Where was there to go? He had already been to the end of the line. His visit to Frieda Blaufeld had only led him to the last of the blank answers.

If only he had come to New York a month earlier! Maybe then his father would have taken him to Mexico with him. Or was it Guatemala? What difference did it make now, Guatemala or Mexico? Bart Brennan had gone on his way, the way of the wind. There was no longer any sense in trying to track him down on the sidewalks and the buildings of New York.

He dressed, finally, and went out to the drugstore in the next block. He bought a magazine and some candy bars and went back to the room. He stayed there all the rest of the morning, reading and eating the candy bars.

By afternoon he was tired of the room. The air smelled close. Anyway, the chambermaid had already knocked on the door four times to ask in a whining voice when she could make up the bed.

He put on his coat and went outside.

He started to walk, without paying much attention to which way he was going. After a while, he found himself at the arched entrance to a large park.

He went through the arch. There were several clutches of mothers with baby carriages sitting on the benches which lined the walks. For the most part, however, the benches were occupied by men who were just sitting there. He could tell from the look of them that they were out of work. Some were reading the want-ad pages of the newspapers with lackluster eyes. Others merely sat with their faces turned emptily toward the sun. Their faces were gray, as though all the blood and hope had been drained out of them. There were even a few young men wearing suits that had been carefully pressed and shoes that carried an expectant shine, even though they had no office to go to. As he passed they looked up with expressions of mild interest, as though they were anxious to talk to him, to anyone. There was no need to scan their faces. He knew now that not one of them could possibly be the face he had come to New York to find.

He spent a nickel on a bag of peanuts and found a place on an empty bench.

For a while he watched the people who passed. Then the squirrels found him. They sat up and looked at him expectantly out of unblinking, obsidian eyes. He held out a few peanuts on his palm and waited to see how close they would dare to come. One actually snatched a peanut from his hand and skittered away up a tree with it. He waited for it to come back, but it didn't. Then the others all darted off. He saw that, a few yards away, an old woman in rusty black clothes and torn sneakers had taken possession of one of the benches and from a brown paper bag was throwing scraps of stale bread to the wheeling pigeons. When the squirrels appeared, she put bits of crust on her shoulders and they scrambled up the back of the bench to get at them.

He watched until the old woman folded her shopping bag and shuffled away, muttering to herself. Then he sat there and ate the rest of the peanuts. When the squirrels came back, there were no more to feed them.

Someone had left a newspaper on the opposite bench. He went and got it. It was yesterday's. He didn't feel like reading it anyway.

Now there was nothing left for him to do but think.

He had a sudden wild idea. He would hitchhike to Mexico!

Almost at once, he shrugged the idea away. Mexico was foreign. To go there you needed a passport. What would be the good of going all that way only to be turned back at the border? And even if he managed to sneak across, where would he start to look, in Mexico? Aah, it was a crazy idea.

If only . . . , he told himself.

If only what?

If only Bart Brennan was like other fathers! Timothy had to face the truth about him at last. What was it Frieda Blaufeld had said? Bart was restless, irresponsible. What was there in his father which made him leave Duffy's Rocks, leave him and Gran? What was there about him which made Aunt Loretta and Aunt Anna exchange those resigned, knowing looks whenever his name was mentioned? Why did he give up job after job, in times like these? Why had he left Marjorie, and then even Frieda Blaufeld? It was as though he was forever running away, and the world was full of people who had loved him and whom he had left behind.

Why?

He crumpled the empty peanut bag and lobbed it into a wastebasket.

Meanwhile, he told himself, he had to decide what he would do. Where could he go from here?

He could join the Navy. He could lie about his age. He was pretty big, after all. Then he would "see the world," as the recruiting posters said. Other boys had done just that.

But he knew he would never get away with it. He still looked too young to enlist.

Or he could stay in New York, panhandling and living from hand to mouth until he found work.

How could he find work, when all those men on the benches around him couldn't?

Suddenly, Timothy felt tired. And he saw that there was a hole in the heel of his left sock.

He instinctively moved his left foot behind the other so that it wouldn't show. His grandmother would never have let him go out with a hole like that in his sock!

At the thought of Gran a wave of longing swept over him. He missed sitting with her in the kitchen. He missed Mr. Kinsella. He even missed the house in Duffy's Rocks. Most of all he missed Gran herself. He ached to see her thin, proud, loving face.

At the same time it seemed peculiar and wrong that, in the middle of a weekday, he was sitting out on a park bench in Brooklyn.

What was he doing here, anyway?

He would never find his father now. He had already found

as much as he ever would. He knew now what his father was like. It was all he could do from this point on to find out who he was himself and what he wanted to be.

The only thing he could be sure of at that moment was that he wanted to go home.

NINETEEN

Duffy's Rocks Again

It was nearly half past nine in the morning when Timothy got off the streetcar and started to walk toward the house. He looked around him. Duffy's Rocks was the same as when he had left it. If anything, it looked even drearier than he remembered. Why should it have changed? He caught a glimpse of Mrs. Sevchick chugging around the corner in her men's shoes, a stick in one hand and Fritzie's leash, with Fritzie tugging impatiently at the end of it, in the other. He was relieved that Mrs. Sevchick hadn't spotted him.

He had come home. It was mortifying to realize that he had returned defeated and alone. Probably, he thought numbly, he would be stuck here in Duffy's Rocks for the rest of his life.

The house was already in sight.

He wondered what he would say to Gran when he went inside. Well, it didn't matter. He would think of something when he saw her. All the same, he braced himself for the sharp edge of her tongue.

There was some consolation—not much, to be sure—in the fact that he could make a quiet entry. Aunt Loretta would be out of the house, at work, and Mary Agnes would long since have left for school. There would be no one but his grand-mother to witness his homecoming.

"Yoo hoo! Timothy!"

The last person on earth he wanted to see just then was Mary Agnes. She loomed in the doorway.

"I was just now looking out of the window, and I saw you coming!" She ran to meet him and danced around him excitedly. "Gee, Timothy, am I glad to see you! I would have written, only I didn't know where to send the letter."

He said sharply, "What are you doing home? Why aren't you in school?"

"I had to stay home today," she said. "On account of Gran."

He came to a halt and stared at her. "What do you mean, on account of Gran?" His face was guarded and apprehensive.

Mary Agnes gulped.

"What's the matter?" he demanded. "Is anything wrong with Gran?"

She nodded importantly.

"She's bad, Timothy. You know Gran. She said she wasn't ready to be taken to any hospital. She told him that she wouldn't and she couldn't, and there was nothing he could do with her."

Timothy pushed passed his cousin and went inside. He set his suitcase on the floor and moved toward the stairs.

"Timothy!" she called after him in a loud whisper. "Where do you think you're going?"

"Up to see her."

"You can't."

He turned slowly.

"Why not?"

"Because you just can't. Dr. Rosenberg's up there now in Gran's room with Mama. He's been here practically all morning."

Timothy considered. "Then I guess I can't," he admitted after a moment. He shifted his direction and went toward the kitchen. Mr. Kinsella was lying on the cushion in Gran's chair, disconsolately licking the fur of his belly.

Mary Agnes trailed after him.

"Timothy?"

"What?"

Her face was flushed with curiosity. "Where did you go?"

"New York," he said.

Her eyes grew wide. "You didn't!"

"I did."

"You could have told me where you were going," she said reproachfully. "I wouldn't have given you away."

"Was Gran wild?"

She thought about it. "No," she said. She giggled. "Mama was. Mama said that you were doing just what your father always did."

"What did Gran say?"

"She was just very quiet. She just sat all the time and didn't say anything. You know something?" she added suddenly. "It's a funny thing. Gran knew that you were coming home today."

"What are you talking about?"

"What I said, that's what. She told Mama yesterday, just before the doctor got here."

Timothy frowned.

"What did she say?"

"Just that. She said, 'I know the boy will be home tomorrow.'"

"When was that?"

"I told you. Yesterday afternoon. I just got back from school. Mrs. Sevchick was here. Gran was in bed and Mrs. Sevchick had called Mama at the Project and made her come right home. Mr. Constantino drove her in his car. Gran was talking kind of funny, in little gasps, like, but I heard every word. She said, 'He should be on his way now.' Mama said she was just rambling. But Gran knew, didn't she?"

Yes, Gran had known that he was coming home. But how, Timothy wondered. It was as though she had been there in the park with him when he made his decision to return.

"Timothy—"

"Now what?"

"What was it like? New York, I mean."

"It was all right," he said.

"Did you see—"

"Look, Mary Agnes," he told her, "I can't talk to you now. For one thing, I'm starving. I rode all night on the bus, and I didn't have anything to eat this morning. I came straight here from the bus station."

"I'll get you something," she volunteered. "You sit down at the table."

As Mary Agnes bustled about the kitchen getting his breakfast, he looked dully around him. Everything was exactly as he had left it. The only thing which was missing was Gran. It didn't seem like her kitchen without her moving about in it, or sitting in her chair rubbing her fingers back and forth on the armrests in the nervous way she had.

Mary Agnes brought him a bowl of Corn Flakes, some milk and sugar, and a banana.

"Is that going to be enough?" she said. "I could fry you some eggs if you want."

He shook his head.

While he ate he kept listening for voices from upstairs. Everything was very quiet. He couldn't hear anything. After a while there was the sound of heavy footsteps on the stairs. Then Dr. Rosenberg's burly shape appeared in the kitchen doorway.

He dumped his bag down on the table. Then he said quietly, "I see the prodigal grandson is back. When did you get here?"

"Just now, Doctor," Timothy said.

"I'm glad to see you got home," he said gravely.

"Can I go up and see her now, Doctor?"

"I guess you can go upstairs to her in a little while," Dr. Rosenberg told him. "I think maybe I ought to have a little talk with you first."

Then Timothy saw Aunt Loretta. She stood in the doorway and looked at him. She didn't say a word.

The doctor cleared his throat.

Aunt Loretta glanced at Mary Agnes. "Come on, Mary Agnes. It's bad enough I have to take off from the Project, but there's no sense in your staying the whole day out of school. You don't want to grow up and be ignorant, do you?"

Mary Agnes tossed her head. "I'm going to be ignorant anyway. I don't learn anything from Sister Veronica."

"That's enough out of you! Grab your books and get going. Anyway, your Aunt Anna should be over any minute."

"Aw, Ma!" Mary Agnes whined. "You said I had to stay home to—"

"You heard me."

Mary Agnes went.

Pointedly, Aunt Loretta said to Dr. Rosenberg, "I'll be up-stairs in case you need me for anything."

"I need you right now, Mrs. Doyle," he said. "I could use a cup of coffee."

"It's all made," she told him. "I'll just heat it up. How do you take it?"

"Milk," he said. "And lots of sugar."

Aunt Loretta went to the stove and fixed his coffee. She set it down on the table and left the room.

Dr. Rosenberg lowered himself into a chair and leaned back. He stirred his coffee a few times, making the spoon clink against the cup. Then he took a long gulp of it. "I needed that," he said. He took another gulp before he turned to Timothy. Then he said, "Well."

Timothy lowered his eyes.

"First of all, it's none of my damned business where you've been," the doctor declared. "But let me tell you one thing. I'm very relieved that you're back."

Timothy remained silent.

"I'd say," he went on, "that if anyone was the apple of your grandmother's eye, it's you." Then he added slowly, "Do you know why she refused to die yesterday?"

Timothy shook his head.

"It was because you hadn't come home yet."

Timothy felt the rush spread over his face. He said huskily, "What do you mean?"

"Just that."

Timothy stared blankly at Mr. Kinsella, whose personal washing had progressed to his white bib.

Dr. Rosenberg took another long, noisy drink of coffee,

emptying the cup. Then he said, "That's why I wanted to talk to you, Timothy, before you went upstairs. I wanted to make sure you didn't come out with anything that might upset her. I won't pussyfoot with you. You're old enough now to face the facts. She's in very critical condition. So play it lightly, if you know what I mean. Just don't let her get excited."

Timothy raised his gaze to Dr. Rosenberg's.

"Is it my fault she's sick? I mean, did it happen because I–?" He broke off. It was difficult for the words to come out.

"No, I don't think so," Dr. Rosenberg replied. "It would have probably have happened anyway, just looking at it in the light of her medical history. I was afraid that it might happen again that time I came—a few months ago, was it? I ought to have insisted that she go to a hospital this time. It's where she ought to be, but she wouldn't hear of it. She told me she couldn't think of dying anywhere except in her own house. But I know she had another reason. She was afraid she might miss you when you came home. That was why I didn't insist on moving her."

"Could you tell me if my grandmother–" Timothy found that it was impossible for him to finish the question.

"Is she going to die this time, you mean?" Dr. Rosenberg said calmly.

Timothy nodded.

Dr. Rosenberg considered. "I don't know, frankly. Mrs. Brennan is a tough old lady. She has always had a fierce hold on life. But in a case like this–" He shrugged and waved his hands in the air. "Who knows? Anyway, I'm doing all I can for her. But the best medicine for your grandmother right now is the fact that you're back home." He rubbed his cheek and surveyed Timothy speculatively. "By the way, now that you've seen the great world, how did you like it?"

It occurred to Timothy at that moment to answer that he had found New York to be a collection of blank boxes which held everything that you could ever want, if only you had the key to open them with. But he hadn't had the key.

But his only reply was to say lamely, "I guess it wasn't all that much different from Duffy's Rocks."

The doctor smiled knowingly at him. "You learned that, anyhow. So it's something," he said. He picked up his coffee cup and raised it to his lips. When he realized that it was empty, he set it down again. Then he took hold of his bag and got up. He gave Timothy a gentle poke in the arm with his heavy hand. "Go upstairs to her now," he told him. "But don't stay with her too long. She needs all her strength if she's going to pull out of this one." He looked at his wristwatch. "Tell your aunt I'll be back this afternoon, as soon as I can get here."

"Yes, I'll tell her."

Aunt Loretta was tiptoeing out of his grandmother's room when he got to the head of the stairs. When she saw Timothy she pulled the door shut behind her.

"The doctor said I could go in," Timothy said.

Without a word to him she opened it again.

Timothy took a deep breath. Then he went in.

TWENTY

Gran

The shades were pulled down all the way to the window sill, and there was an unfamiliar smell in the room, sweetish and faintly disagreeable.

Timothy advanced slowly through the dimness toward the bed where his grandmother was. Her inert hands lay on top of the bedclothes. They looked as thin as tissue paper.

He felt a little nervous about being there all alone. He almost wished that Aunt Loretta had come with him. He stood over the bed and peered down at his grandmother. She looked very small, as though she had been crumpled. She did not move. Her eyes were closed. He couldn't even be sure that she was breathing. He began to panic. Was she dead? He stretched out a hand to take one of hers, but even before he touched it she said without opening her eyes and in a voice which he had to hold his breath to hear, "Tim?"

"I'm here, Gran," he said in a hoarse whisper. "I'm back."

"I knew it," she said with an effort. "I waited for you."

"I know."

"Let me look at you."

Her eyelids fluttered open. Her eyes looked bleached.

He took her hand then, and its fingers clutched his in a grip which surprised him with its strength. She'll be all right now, he thought. He loved her so much that he could hardly bear to look at her.

With her free hand she made an incomplete gesture toward the chair. She would not let go her hold on him, but he managed to pull the chair to the bedside. He sat there, bending forward toward her, uncomfortably balanced, feeling the pressure of her bony fingers.

He thought that she would ask him where he had gone, but she only moved her lips into the phantom of a smile. It made her look grotesque. He realized that it was because her false teeth were out of her mouth. He could glimpse them through the murk, sitting in a glass on the table next to the bed.

"You'll get well soon, Gran," he told her.

She did not say anything. She only shook her head from side to side, smiling fixedly at him, and pressing his hand tighter, as though to reassure him that she knew the truth and that it didn't matter anymore.

"Dr. Rosenberg said so," he added.

She took a harsh breath. "The time comes," she whispered, "when there's suddenly an end, and you haven't the strength to start again." It was hard to understand all the words. He supposed that it was because of her teeth being out.

"Don't say that, Gran!"

"It's better to wear out, Tim, than to rust."

"Ah, Gran!"

She fell silent for a moment. Then she closed her eyes for an instant.

"I'm so tired, Tim. So incredibly tired."

"Come on, Gran. That's no way to talk," he said desperately. "You can't leave me, Gran."

"I don't want to die until you grow up. That's God's truth. I don't want to leave you," she said. His hand hurt from the sudden spurt of pressure from hers. She fell silent again. After a moment she stirred. Her mouth opened and closed without any sound coming out of it.

He leaned closer. He could hear the chair creak under him.

"Is there anything you want to tell me?" he asked her.

"Just that you'll be a good boy," she said.

He couldn't help smiling.

"I will, Gran. I promise."

"I don't want you to be like your father. Listen to me, Tim." Her voice was like the rustling of paper. "I want you to make something of yourself, to be a real man. God forgive me, I was too indulgent with your father. I let him go his own way all the time, and he threw his life away on will-o'-the-wisps, chasing the moon, thinking all the time that the world owed him a living. I want you to have the will not to go to waste. Promise me that."

"Yes, Gran," he said.

He sat there holding her hand. She closed her eyes. The battered clock on the dresser ticked like thunder. Suddenly, her eyes sprang open again.

"Who was that at the door?"

He turned to look.

"It's no one, Gran."

"I thought it was your grandfather," she said, "coming home from work and the supper not ready."

"No, Gran."

She smiled again. "I forgot he was gone," she said. Her smile was no longer grotesque, but faint and like a child's. "I'm letting go, Tim."

"No, Gran. Hold on to me."

"You're all I have to hold on to, Tim. You're the only one left who needs me. I wouldn't mind going, except for you."

"You're not going anywhere, Gran," he insisted stubbornly. "You're going to get well and live to dance a jig at my wedding."

Her shallow breath came out in a low sigh.

"I'm too tired, Tim. The days of the Kerry dancing was finished a long time ago. Just sit here with me for a small minute before you go."

"Do you want anything?" he asked after a while. "Should I get Aunt Loretta?"

She shook her head. "I just want to sleep. I feel so tired. What time is it?"

"It's still morning."

"Morning?" She seemed surprised. "Ah, but it would be for you, Tim." She closed her eyes. "You leave me now," she said.

Timothy disengaged his hand from hers. Her fingers seemed to be reluctant to release him. Her hand moved sketchily against the covers, as though she meant to wave good-bye.

"You get a good rest, Gran," he told her.

"Yes," she said.

He stumbled out of the room and left her there alone in the dark.

TWENTY-ONE

After the Rosary

I t was all over.

Timothy was leaving Duffy's Rocks.

But this time it was not as he had planned. And he was not running off into the great world.

He sat in the parlor, the suitcases with everything he owned all packed and lined up beside him, and Mr. Kinsella in his lap. The house had been sold. Uncle Matt had arranged it all very quickly. Most of the furniture was already gone: a few things, including the china set, to Aunt Anna's house; some of it with Aunt Loretta, who was going to take Mary Agnes to live with that divorced friend of hers for a while until Mr. Patsy Constantino found a suitable house for them, after which they were going to be married. Mary Agnes was looking forward to living with her mother's friend, whose daughter was just the same age and whose name was Gloria. As for her mother's marrying Mr. Constantino, Mary Agnes only flung back her mane of gypsy hair and said, "Ish-kabibble!"

What was left of the furniture was going to be picked up some time before the house's new owner took possession. Uncle Matt had taken care of that, too. A second-hand dealer he knew was taking it off their hands: the parlor sofa, the kitchen table and chairs, the dining room furniture, everything. He had said that it was old-fashioned junk that nobody wanted anymore, but as a special favor to Uncle Matt he would give them fifty dollars for the lot, all cash. Aunt Anna said, what could they have done with the stuff? There was no room for it in her house. Uncle Matt said that in these times you couldn't turn up your nose at cash. The fifty dollars, along with the money from the house, would go for Tim's education. It was what Gran would have wanted.

It seemed to Timothy that everything had happened very quickly in the week since his grandmother died.

She had gone during the night. He had not seen her again after the morning he had come home. It was as though she had waited to see him before permitting herself to die.

The funeral had been splendid, everything as Gran would have liked it. Uncle Matt saw to that. Father Halloran said the rosary. Everyone was there, including Dr. Rosenberg. The only bad part was when Mrs. Sevchick embarrassed the family at the cemetery with her loud, uncontrolled weeping. But, as they all said, Mrs. Sevchick was a foreigner

And now it was all finished.

Aunt Loretta and Mary Agnes had left in Mr. Constantino's car half an hour before to go to their temporary home, and Timothy was waiting for Uncle Matt to pick him up. He was going to live with Uncle Matt and Aunt Anna. He would have his own room in their house. He wondered how he would get on with Regis and Leo. He would manage, he supposed.

The house was very still now. It was as empty as he felt. He had a feeling of having been deserted and abandoned in it. For the moment, he was almost angry with Gran for having left him. He thought of his trip to New York, the fruitless hunt for his father. He hadn't found him. But at least he had found out that he would have to live without the dream of finding him. Maybe that, he decided, was a kind of a beginning.

From outside, an automobile horn tooted.

A moment later, Uncle Matt appeared.

"Are you ready, Tim?"

Timothy gripped a suitcase in one hand and Mr. Kinsella in the other. He got to his feet.

"I'll take the rest," Uncle Matt said, gathering up the other suitcases as though they were mere grocery packages. "You haven't left anything behind, have you?"

Timothy shook his head.

"You'd better make sure."

Timothy looked around for the last time. His eye caught something hanging on the wall. It was the framed motto: "An Irish Blessing," with its shamrocks and its imitation Celtic script.

May the road rise to meet you. May the wind be always at your back. May the sun shine warm upon your face, the rains fall soft upon your fields, and, until we meet again, may God hold you in the palm of His hand.

The words were as familiar to him as his grandmother's face.

He took it down from the wall and tucked it carefully under his arm.

Then he turned to Uncle Matt.

"I'm ready," he said. "I guess."

Afterword

Duffy's Rocks is clearly modeled after McKees Rocks, only five minutes from downtown Pittsburgh. The setting of McKees Rocks, the Depression, and the varied ethnic immigrant groups add color and depth to the story of Timothy Brennan and his struggle to come to terms with his father's disappearance. In the 1930s, at the time this story takes place, nearly 19,000 people lived in the Rocks. Today less than half that number live there, but some residents still remember the Great Depression and what the times were like.

The author, Edward Fenton (1917–1995), never lived in Pittsburgh, but it is said that a friend invited him there for a wedding. From that visit and discussions about the friend's childhood, the story for Timothy Brennan took shape. Fenton's books are all notable for a strong sense of place and character, including those he translated from other languages.

The book has been unavailable for years, but the story rings so true that it is time to bring it back to be enjoyed by new readers. The University of Pittsburgh Press has made this effort because young readers are part of the Press's mission to publish books that contribute to our understanding of Pittsburgh and western Pennsylvania and to serve the needs of the whole community. (A few emendations have been made to the text to meet the needs of today's young readers.)

Parents and teachers may want to investigate with young readers the many other stories, biographies, and histories of the Great Depression. Many rich resources are available to add perspective to Brennans' life. The Internet also provides a multitude of sites that provide access to photos, music, and the sound of the times.

Connections to other books, videos, and websites will be available to anyone who wishes to wander farther along the rivers and in the hills surrounding Pittsburgh in a website at the University of Pittsburgh Press. Look at *http://www.pitt.edu/ ~press/goldentrianglebooks* for *Duffy's Rocks.*